a far time

a far time

j.a. wainwright

mosaic press

Canadian Cataloguing in Publication Data

Wainwright, J.A., 1946-
  A far time

ISBN 0-88962-759-2 (bound) ISBN 0-88962-758-4 (pbk)

I. Title.

PS8595.A54F37 2001   C813'.54   C00-933267-7
Pr9199.3.W34F37 2001

Published by Mosaic Press, offices and warehouse at 1252 Speers Road, Units 1 and 2, Oakville, Ontario, L6L 5N9, Canada and Mosaic Press, PMB 145, 4500 Witmer Industrial Estates, Niagara Falls, NY, 14305-1386, U.S.A.

Mosaic Press acknowledges the assistance of the Canada Council and the Department of Canadian Heritage, Government of Canada for their support of our publishing programme.

Copyright © 2001 J.A. Wainwright
ISBN 0-88962-759-2 HC, ISBN 0-88962-758-4 PB
Printed and Bound in Canada.

MOSAIC PRESS, in Canada:
1252 Speers Road, Units 1 & 2,
Oakville, Ontario
L6L 5N9
Phone/Fax: 905-825-2130
mosaicpress@on.aibn.com

MOSAIC PRESS, in U.S.A.:
4500 Witmer Industrial Estates
PMB 145, Niagara Falls, NY
14305-1386
Phone/Fax: 1-800-387-8992
mosaicpress@on.aibn.com

Le Conseil des Arts   The Canada Council
du Canada   for the Arts

for the quartet

Where there are ghosts, there is always hunger;
for the life unlived the knot that draws desire
back; something unresolved and ongoing.

— Daphne Marlatt

A saxophone someplace far-off played

— Bob Dylan

PRELUDE

In the Avila town square, the tourists sipped their *cafés con leché*, and turned their faces to a sea breeze that barely rustled the leaves of the plane trees. Fortunately they were in the shade of the trees because the mid-afternoon sun beat down on the stones of the square, forcing even the pigeons to take modest shelter, and the boy who had served them salad and bread to don a baseball cap against the heat.

Some of them were from the tour buses that lined the main road, but a few had driven to Avila in rented cars where the international conference on food distribution in third-world countries had concluded its week-long meetings. Ibiza had been chosen as the site of this year's meetings because of strong lobbying by a Spanish government eager to promote its economic interests in impoverished areas of Central America, which meant virtually the entire region south of the Rio Grande. The Balearic Islands were conveniently located between the nations of the European and African delegates, and were more or less equidistant from North America and Asia—that was the argument, at least, with the emphasis on Ibiza as a charming venue without the distractions of the other islands, especially the Club-Med atmosphere of Formentera.

One of the delegates had spent several years as an aid worker in Guatemala. Her subsequent experience as a UNESCO administrator, as well as her public-speaking abilities, had led her to many such conferences where worthy individuals discussed worthwhile causes, and brought forward motions intended to effect change in the world order, only to have their efforts undermined by the forces of corporate globalization. Two steps forward, she thought; it was the only way to keep going. A number of good things had been accomplished here; among them a resolution that called on elected Guatemalan officials to end army interference in the allotment of foreign aid to the Mayans in different parts of the country. Since the last military dictatorship and the horrific campaign of violence conducted against Guatemala's indigenous peoples, the *ladino* commanders of the armed forces were carrying out economically-based vendettas whose impact was a fierce follow-up to the genocide that she had witnessed at first-hand. Barely protected by her American citizenship, the same citizenship held by the State Department advisors she loathed, she had looked on helplessly as lives and culture in the district in which she worked were eradicated in the name of God and democracy. She carried devastating memories with her to every podium and discussion table where she fought in the gap between audience privilege and the continuing Mayan pain she attempted to alleviate with words.

Karen put one hand up to brush a strand of hair from her cheek, and her fingers grazed the dreamcatcher earrings flecked with silver and blue that she had bought as a teenager from a Native woman in Eureka. In those days, she had rarely asked any questions about the 'Indians' around her, had not spoken to any of them except to barter over trinkets that acquired value through association with dying creative expression. Yet so much of her response to the landscape of her childhood, and to the high mountain mists of Baja

Verapaz when the guns were quiet, was bound up in that Costanoan saying *Noso'n*, 'in breath as it is in spirit.' She had been back to Central America more times than she had returned to California, to the beach of rocks and surf an hour's drive from Ferndale, where the sea pulsed through her veins and 'home' was in everything she could see and touch. It had been nearly a decade since she had walked the tide-line, watching the gannets wheel and plunge, and the bobbing kelp-heads that barked in the early morning light. The rock at the end of the beach reminded her vaguely of the one she had climbed with Jake at Big Sur in the sixties. How young and crazy they had been. Wherever he was, she hoped he was happy.

I

BIG SUR

Once she wrote him,

I'm home, and wondering how much surroundings affect people. It was sunny for three days. Now it's foggy, and I'm lying on the couch looking out at the gray and the green oak light. A strange feeling of solitude and a still world, and life is vibrant and beautiful, though part sad in a transparent eggshell. I can hear music, across the street, in a passing car. It's as though you're here. Certainly I feel you more in the fog than in L.A. where everything seems so one-dimensional. I wonder what would happen if we were a daily reality to one another. I'm scared of all I say to you.

How could he write about Cape Mendocino and what it meant to him? The Lost Coast road curved through pine forests on its way to the sea. It was paved, but very narrow, and because it was April there were no other cars. Once a mule deer skittered in front of him, and an occasional hawk sailed across the blue gap between the trees. He was alone in California, as he had been twenty years before. There hadn't been very much to think about then, to puzzle over, to answer for.

The conference in Arcata had been interesting, not least because Jake had met several Australians who knew his work and had invited him on a tour down under. He had read some poems about Ibiza and the tiny *finca* in the center of the island, and then a few passages from the California section of the novel-in-progress. The audience had been appreciative, asking questions afterwards about the relationship between his life and writing, questions that he did try to answer, but with an evasiveness that had become second nature to him now. He wasn't sure of the relationship, or where the novel was taking him. His life wasn't confirmed by creative expression the way it used to be. Originally he had intended to go back to Montreal when the conference was finished, and work on the novel through the summer, before the new teaching term began when he would have to assess the portfolios of the many students who came to him with their stories and poems.

The coastline north of Arcata was rocky and wild. The conference banquet had been held at an old inn a few feet above high tide mark, and a fierce thunder and lightning storm had played above the surf pounding on the reefs offshore. The sand and sky reminded him unmistakably of the beach on Big Sur and the huge rock he had climbed with Karen that summer.

They met on a blind date in London where he was trying to make ends meet by writing book reviews for newspapers and magazines. It had taken him a long time to convince editors that, despite being Canadian, he had a valid degree in English literature and was widely-read. The first book he got was Dee Brown's *Bury My Heart at Wounded Knee*, the idea being, he supposed, that anyone who had grown up within a thousand miles of a reservation was bound to know more Indians than an Oxford don or a member of the London literary crowd.

A friend told him about the younger acquaintance of a woman he was taking to dinner.

-How much younger?-

-Seventeen.-

That meant three years between them, and he wasn't too happy about the prospect, but his friend had been good to him, letting him stay rent-free in his Knightsbridge flat for several months, so he said yes. They all went out to dinner together, and then to a John Gielgud play near Picadilly Circus.

Karen was just out of a California high school, but seemed much older than the girls who had sat in the front row of his university classes, taking notes on Leonard Cohen as if censorship were just around the corner. Jake liked her quick mind, the banter that went back and forth between them about American jingoism and Canadian nationalism, and he liked the way her fingers made soft circles of indentation on the tablecloth as she spoke, digits of purpose and grace that prefigured her movement in a college gymnasium or a lover's arms.

In the following week, when she wasn't with her mother or aunt, they spent short evenings together, walking, talking, and holding hands through Hyde Park, or kissing on benches in Sloane Square after dark when the two guardians had retired. They didn't sleep together. At the time he told himself it was her youth that held him back, but afterwards he realized it was a choice she had made. When she left London to visit France and then return to the States, he felt abandoned, although her letters suggested she wouldn't entirely disappear from his life.

Paris was incredible. We stayed in the apartment of a friend of my aunt, and discovered we had landed in a hotbed of rabid conservatives. I was fascinated by the whole experience. These people lived and breathed politics. They were all editors and journalists and evidently had a fair portion of underground political power. They hated DeGaulle with a passion exceeded only by their love of France, hated him to an extent that it was hinted they were involved in a plot against his life. They had fought in the Algerian revolt and felt that DeGaulle had sold them out. They still firmly believed in France's destiny as conceived by Napoleon, and all I could feel in them was tragedy.

...I have this image of life and involvement. Either you are free, like a bird that can feel its own strength and every beat of its wings as it flies above the sea of life, and so rejoices in the sea's splendor and its own; or else you're totally involved, you are life, are the sea, and distinctions are impossible because you're living your whole existence. Where does that leave us, you and I? It's hard to tell if life is not just a series of frustrated relationships, and if each new relationship grows out of a frenzy to somehow perfect the old. I suppose there is a beauty to the release people find in one another.

Jake went home to Toronto, and worked several nights a week in a downtown record store. In addition to half-price albums by Dylan and Archie Shepp, he had enough cash in hand to share a three-bedroom apartment in the tree-lined Annex near the university. He and Karen wrote to each other every few weeks. She was at Vassar in her freshman year, and more than once he tried to telephone.

I was so mad at missing your call. I should have been quietly drinking myself to death in my room, or slitting my wrists, or hanging wretchedly in my closet. I have this frightening feeling at times that I was just too weak to give religion a chance. I hate not knowing where I am.

Vassar has a reputation of being a proving-ground for political types, but I haven't found that at all. Everyone I know well is rather disappointingly wholesome. I think I expected to come here and find some glorious communion of minds. Perfection obviously does not occur that simply. The head of our Philosophy Department is one of the best teachers I've ever had. He also offers silent film seminars every week or so in which he plays fast piano to accompany Chaplin, Harold Lloyd, etc. His hair is all over the place, and he looks like he could have stepped out of a Mack Sennett chase scene.

In the late spring of 1967 he decided to go to California. Karen would be there for the summer holidays, maybe in Los Angeles, maybe at home in Ferndale in the north of the state. They had both been involved with others in the last year, which was only part of the reason why he hadn't gone down to Poughkeepsie. Though he never talked about the impact of distance and time, she didn't shy away.

I don't know whether you care or not, but just in case, I've been going with a guy here and he may be in California some of the summer. However, that doesn't mean I don't want to see you. To the contrary, it means that I'm already confused about the whole situation. Periodically I inform myself that I really scarcely know you, and to constantly be relating things to this strange feeling I have about you, and whatever is between us, is insane because I can't navigate, or expect to, on the basis of some dreamy reservation. Basically I wonder if it is possible or right to feel something for another person you never see or hardly know, or if some people just have a fantastic ability to build air castles which they impose upon themselves...lousy metaphor!

It was San Francisco that appealed to him. He wanted to see Haight-Ashbury and share in the scene he'd read about in *Time* and *Newsweek*, though he wasn't a communal person, and was usually monogamous during his short-term relationships. A month before Karen was due to finish her year at Vassar, Jake took a bus to Buffalo and flew standby to the west coast. He didn't have a job, and couldn't work legally in California without a permit, but he was sure something would turn up. At the downtown YMCA he made the mistake of getting into a poker game with some rough characters, including a Vietnam vet who never stopped smiling. They cleaned him out, all but twenty dollars American that would last him for a couple of days, no more.

The next morning he wandered down to the marina within sight of the Golden Gate Bridge, and asked a man painting his cabin cruiser if anyone was hiring casual labour.

The man squinted at him in the bright sunlight.-Name's Frank. Can you paint?-

Jake stepped on board for the next two weeks, scraping

the rails and sanding them before applying the varnish, holding on to the bow rail as the boat bobbed up and down, slapping grey deck paint in hard-to-reach places. He got fifty a week under the table, and stayed away from card games.

When the work on the boat was done, Frank offered him a job cleaning up his apartment complex in Palo Alto, thirty miles south. He didn't have much choice, but things turned out well. He lived in a furnished basement room at Frank's house, and had meals with him and his wife. Their daughter, who was engaged to a Stanford graduate, kept her distance once she discovered his blond hair and blue eyes weren't Californian but part of some strange stock north of New York State. For the first time in his life Jake felt rather primitive. This feeling was compounded one weekend afternoon when he hitchhiked down to Santa Clara to a rock concert and was picked up by a teenager in a Mustang who immediately asked him what was wrong with his wheels. It was then he realized that the kids he saw every morning on their way to the local collegiate were driving their own cars. While they were in class he worked in and around the apartment buildings, cutting lawns, hauling trash, painting doorways and window frames for the same amount of requisite cash.

Sometimes he went across town to the Stanford campus and played touch football with tall, sun-kissed young men who looked as if they came from the same expensive home. They were very good and very fast, and not much he could do with feints or patterns perturbed them. Later he saw them coming out of their medical exams for the

Army or Marines, some of them raising clenched fists in exaltation, others weeping with relief at having been classified 4-F with trick knees or flat feet that had never affected their football prowess. Vietnam was a bird of madness that brushed by him without notice, and hovered at the shoulders of those with fists in the air who had yet to step ashore at Danang. They knew nothing of war that could be distinguished from the John Wayne heroics of their childhood movie screens. While those who wept spurned the camera eye to read a darker script in which the Duke was fiction to the end, and turned away from the celebrants as from a forbidden book of the dead.

Two months passed. In the mornings Jake rode his bicycle to the apartment and waved at the kids in their cars. For lunch he usually walked several blocks to the local taco takeout and sat at a picnic table in the sun. Frank's wife insisted he eat supper with them, and he did because the cooking was so good, and the generous salads offset the taco diet. There was no hurry about anything in that house, but Denise, the daughter, had her own kind of speed as she ignored him on her way out to a weekend date or told her parents about her classes at Foothills Junior College just down the highway.

He went to films on Saturday nights. At the local theatre he saw the Michael Caine sequel to *The Ipcress File* and an Elvis flick, and in a folk club that had movies on Thursday evenings, along with free popcorn and large steins of beer, he saw Bogart and Bacall in *Key Largo*. He read Raymond Chandler novels and a new book by Richard Farina that anticipated the West Coast cultural explosion of the coming summer. His fifty dollars lasted all week, He insisted on giving ten of it back to Frank for food, and after the tacos the rest was for beer and music. He bought a small record player and the albums of the groups that were beginning to emerge—the Airplane, Country Joe, the Dead. At Stanford pot was cheap; he would carry it back to the house in a paper bag, light a candle, open the basement window, and lie back beneath a smoky cloud to listen to "White Rabbit" or anything by Tim Buckley.

One night there was a knock on the door. Jake panicked. Frank's place and the job were too valuable to lose.

-It's me- said Denise.

Surprised, but relieved, he unlocked the door. She came in and sat, in tight jeans and t-shirt, on the edge of his bed, her amazingly white teeth reflecting all the light in his subterranean den.

-I was doing a laundry. The smell is pretty strong out there.-

He passed her the toke, and she inhaled it deftly. -Not bad. Where'd you get it?-

-Hey, you might be a narc, for all I know.-

-If I were you'd be up shit creek now.-

-Yeah, okay. Let's start again. Is that a roach in your pocket, or are you just happy to see me?-

She laughed. -I haven't been exactly friendly, have I? But I'm almost a married woman, after all.-

-*Girls by the whirlpool, lookin' for the new fool.*-

-What?-

-Dylan.-

-Oh. So tell me about Canada.-

-What do you want to know?- He was getting tired of this. Fooling around with her would certainly lose him the house and job, but pretty soon they were going to run out of conversation.

He had called Karen twice at Vassar. It was strange talking to her from her home state, and from thousands of miles farther away than he had been in Toronto. She had to go to L.A. for a summer job her uncle had arranged in a bank, but would try to come north for a long weekend. By then he wasn't sure who or what he was waiting for. It was almost a year since they had been together. They had never traded photos, and it was hard to remember the exact shape of her nose or colour of her hair, hard especially to recall how she had moved beside him in the Hyde Park twilight. But he knew her voice because of the phone conversations, and it held him to her through the intervening space and time. He could hear it in her letters, and the way she said *out* and *about* with a nasal twang, accusing him of pronouncing them *oot* and *aboot*, or spoke so disparagingly of Lyndon Johnson and the War.

Last week I went to an anti-War demonstration in New York where LBJ came to drum up support for his next campaign with a $500 a plate dinner. I didn't expect much, but there was a turnout of about twenty thousand. What affected me was the behaviour of the cops. I won't go into details, but they acted as if we were in a police state. They used a lot of unnecessary force, and obviously had their orders. They gave *no clear warning before they charged into us, and their actions were aimed at control, not justice, rights, or freedom. There is so much in this country that needs correction.*

...shades of London. New York has some wonderful little nuances of it. I thought about you often. The Central Park Zoo has a clock that chimes every half hour, and little crazy bronze animals come out to dance around it to music while monkeys hit the chimes with hammers.

-So do you have a girlfriend up there?-

A farm girl, he thought, in baggy jeans, who cooks flap-jacks for the hired hands. -She's younger than you.-

-Still in high school?- She smiled and put out her hand for the toke.

-Actually she goes to Vassar, and is in L.A. this summer.-

-You mean she's from California?- The tone of alarm was barely discernable, but it was there.

-Born and bred. But what's the difference? You came to see me, didn't you?- He passed her the toke.

She stood up. -No, thanks. I've got to go. The laundry will be dry by now.- How long had she stood in the basement before deciding to come slumming?

-You know your way *oot*.- When she had closed the door behind her, Jake wet his index finger with his tongue and made an invisible mark in the air. I'm a prick, he thought, but at least I'm Canadian.

He didn't know what arrangements he would make for Karen's accomodation. Frank's house was out of the question. He couldn't break the same house rules that applied to Denise. Since he didn't much like the idea of a cheap hotel in Palo Alto or San Francisco, he was happy when Karen called from L.A. to suggest they stay with some of her friends near Monterey, and attend a three-day rock festival together.

Monterey was just north of Big Sur where Robinson Jeffers had lived in his Yeatsian stone tower and written fierce narrative poems about women, hills, and horses, not to mention the Pacific breaking against the continent like a lost voice. "Tamar," in particular, was one Jake remembered, with its sensuous, sweetly-dark images of loss, revenge, and death. Big Sur was also where Joan Baez hung out, her romance with Dylan apparently over. Though she no longer appeared in concert with him, she still sang his songs, and was writing her own about the politics of love and war. Richard Farina had been her brother-in-law when he died in a motorcycle crash the previous winter.

Jake hitchhiked along the inland highway to Monterey, and waited at the town's airport for Karen's plane to arrive. When he saw her walking across the tarmac, her reddish-brown hair whipping in the wind and disguising her face, he wondered for a moment if it was all a mistake. What if they had nothing more to say, once the few days in London had been recalled, and what if the physical spark couldn't be rekindled, leaving one or both of them cold and embarrassed? She was eighteen now and he was twenty-one. Did that close or widen the distance between them? Two different countries, he thought, and two lovers for him. How many trips to New York City for her, where Columbia boys and Greenwich Village attractions awaited the Vassar clientele? No, that was a cheap shot. There had been the specific "guy" back east who was with her now in L.A. But she had accepted Jake's trip to California without qualm and, in their communications, like him, had always seemed drawn to the inevitability of their meeting again.

On the height of land above Cape Mendocino, before the road dropped to the sea, he pulled over and got out of the car. The gravel by the pavement was reddish-brown and mixed with pine needles that glistened with early morning dew. The ticking of the engine was the only sound. He listened for birds, but heard none, while the surf broke silently on the rocks at least five miles to the west and far below.

Dear Karen:

Remember "Wild Thing" by The Troggs? They have a new song out now with a refrain that asks, "Will you dance with me." Why do I think of you when I hear it? We never danced, did we? In the high school gym I watched all the beauty queens from higher grades spin by me in the arms of boys I insisted were merely older versions of myself. How I wanted to hold them, but turned from that impossibility to playing disk jockey in a time when no one thought of bringing in local bands. There I was in a corner by the washroom doors, with a portable turntable and its built-in speaker. They would come to me with 78s of Elvis or Bobby on, a dreamy look in their eyes that didn't see me at all, and I would play their requests. "For Paul, from Sarah," the obscenities inches from my lips.

Years later, in Greece, Sarah would tell him again how unhappy she had been as a teenager, and when he reminded her how she had figured in his wet dreams, she laughed and asked why he hadn't called her.

-I did. Your mother or brother always answered. It's amazing how often you weren't home.-

Karen's friends lived on the coast in Carmel, a few miles from Monterey. It was an imaginary kind of place with its dirt roads and multi-storied wooden houses among trees that grew to enormous heights, levering themselves through wrap-around decks like untrimmed masts, their upper branches in full and trembling sail before the wind. The mother and father lived in self-contained fashion on higher floors, so they shared a large space below with two teenage sisters and their younger brother, Karen in one bedroom with the girls, and him in the other with a ten-year-old and his posters of Tolkein. Jake wasn't really focused on the boy, but they did have several exchanges about dwarves and dragons with weak spots, and how magic could save the world. Once he asked him if Golem wasn't always getting the short end of the stick, and received an affronted stare by way of reply, as if the line between heroes and villains was always visible in the sand.

He and Karen spent the first night talking, while the parents and siblings went off to the opening of the rock festival. About Vassar, trimmed and cultivated like an English country estate, with fences to keep out the locals, and about Toronto, whose British enclaves felt increasingly threatened by what they saw as Mediterranean, eastern European, and Caribbean neighbourhoods sprawling loosely and noisly north of the lake without regard for the demarcated past. He told her of his boyhood in the west end of the city among the Italian, Lithuanian, and Jewish families, and how he had always naively considered Canada a mixture of peoples, even though he never met any Blacks or Indians in public or high school. When young, he hadn't given any thought to the former, and even on civil rights marches in university, in response to Birmingham and Selma, he never asked himself about their presence as a force in *Canadian* society. As for Native peoples, for too long he had assumed they kept to themselves by choice on rural reserves.

In turn, she told him about Ferndale, the gateway to the Lost Coast, with its ornate nineteenth-century houses and main street hotel where Bret Harte had lived for many years. The town was very small, and the real Saturday night excitement was to get a ride over to Eureka, about twenty miles away, and cruise the strip there or hang around the Blue Bird club with its tiny stage, where Oregon bands on their way to Frisco sometimes stopped. There were a few Blacks in Eureka, families of men who worked in mountain lumber camps, and many more Indians, some of whom slouched in bar doorways while others set up stalls of leather goods and jewelry for the tourists who came through between the end of May and early September.

-I bought these in Eureka.- she said, pulling back her hair to reveal the dreamcatcher earrings flecked with silver and blue -but I never thought about who made them or where they lived. I should have.-

And Jake said, yes, it had been the same with him when once he'd found a leather vest in a second-hand store, sewn with beaded symbols he had not tried to interpret. -I wore it everywhere until I wore it out. I guess I always thought of it as western gear, something belonging to a hip gun-slinger in Dodge City.-

Karen laughed. -Do you still have it?-

-In a closet or a box in my parents' basement.-

-I'd like to see it.-

The distance was immeasurable between them, but he crossed it, took her hand in his, and kissed her. He wanted to say things like *I missed you* or *I love you*, but because they were stupid things to say to someone you didn't really know, he didn't say anything. He felt very close to her, perhaps because of the tenuousness of their relationship, and be-cause, despite the intensity with which they spoke and touched now, there didn't seem to be any possible future to it. She was going back to L.A. and he, sooner or later, would return to Toronto where his history was. She must have felt the pull of her own history because they drew back simul-taneously, and stood up, straightening their clothes, smil-ing apologetically as if they had been caught at something slightly illegal.

-It's not easy.-

-No, but I don't think we should let that beat us. We still have three days.- She turned toward the door. -Let's go out and get something to eat.-

They walked down the dirt road to the village square without holding hands. There were no streetlights, and it was very dark and quiet except for the stars and the sound of the waves on the beach. Just before they got to the corner where the café sign flickered, Jake heard the stupid words, and thought at first it was his own voice betraying him.

-I love you. I don't know why. And it doesn't make any sense. We haven't been together for more than a few hours in our lives, and we've talked on the phone a few times. It's not going to last. It can't. I have a boyfriend in L.A., and I'm sleeping with him. I know you're with someone, or maybe more than one. It all belongs in a book somewhere.- She took his hand and pulled him toward the light.

After decades he would still remember how they drank coffee and ate ice cream, and didn't talk about their lovers, but about Dylan and the Band, who were all, save one, Canadian. They didn't know the lead guitarist, Robbie Robertson, was from the Six Nations Reserve since Robbie wasn't letting on in those days. Karen mentioned a black guitarist from Seattle named Hendrix who was supposed to play the next night.

The festival was held in an old rodeo arena in Monterey. The grounds outside were covered with tents and tarpaulins and three-legged barbecues that reminded Jake of the summer Sundays when his father had cooked dinner in the backyard. He'd been to the Haight, so he wasn't surprised by the long hair and beads that were everywhere and made him nostalgic for the leather vest, or by the home-grown aroma that seemed like a real alternative to fresh air. What did surprise him were the many cops, at least the ones in uniform who walked stiffly in stolid blue among the colours of the crowd, pistols on their hips, batons swinging like short baseball bats made for the right-field fence.

At the time he didn't realize this was the first outdoor rock concert of such a size anywhere, and the several thousand hippies, wannabees, and just plain folks gathered there were the largest group of rock fans ever assembled for more than an afternoon or evening bash. On this basis, the authorities must have thought there was bound to be trouble, and besides, some of the plain folks, when you focused through the fragrant haze, were bikers; the Harleys straining madly, as if on a leash the boys in black held at their pleasure while beer bottles flashed in the sun. But nothing exploded. Before the music began, politics were fairly local, the War was at a distance, and peace was still a concept that could be contained in a two-finger signal, or in smiles coruscating more often than bottles across the multitudinous space.

Hendrix was the headline. Wiring *The Star-Spangled Banner* to the sky and burning his guitar, the psychedelic voodoo child put a hex on America and gave his music to the brothers in the rice paddies and on the jungle trails, transforming as he did so white crackers with names like Billy Bob, midwestern flatttops called Ray, New England boys whose fathers would back Nixon despite their Democratic Party roots, running a razored riff across the high sweet sounds of Michelle, Cass, John, and Denny who harmonized farewell to the first golden era of rock 'n roll and their brief time at the top.

But it was a small woman Jake had never heard of, her hair cutting the air like a bullwhip, her legs charged with sexual energy, and her voice burning like a Zippo flame beneath a thatched roof, who told them all that nothing was the same anymore. She came on with Big Brother and the Holding Company on Saturday afternoon, when half the crowd was sleeping off the night before, and launched into *Ball and Chain*. Everybody ducked. Mama Cass stared up at Janis Joplin from the front row, her eyes popping with wonder, her mouth breathing life into the stone-dead hippie term, "Wow!" He and Karen were farther back, but knew what they were seeing and hearing was original. There were no words that could say it any better than Cass's lone monosyllable of praise. Only later, back in Toronto, did he try to tell others about the birth of a sound that gutted the rules with such reckless disregard, while drawing instinctively, powerfully, tenderly, on every blues record available in East Texas in the early sixties. The concert moguls brought Janis back for the Sunday night finale in sequined disarray. "Take another little piece of my heart," she urged the crowd. And it did.

They shared a toke handed to them by a happy kid who in the dizzy night vibration seemed to have tie-dyed his naked upper torso in rainbow colours. A Mamas and Papas protégé was on stage giving flowery advice about going to San Francisco. The next morning they borrowed a car from the Carmel family, threw in a knapsack, a couple of sleeping bags, and some wine, and drove to Big Sur.

-The Carmelite monks had monasteries overlooking the sea. They rode horses on the beaches, and gave shelter to travellers and drowned sailors.-

-Drowned sailors?-

-Shipwrecked, I mean. This coast was deadly. There was a lot of trade, even before the gold rush.-

-Captain Cook claimed it all for England, I think, though the Spanish had something to say about that. And George Vancouver, another English captain, lost crew who went AWOL and probably ended up with the monks for awhile. It must have been beautiful then. It's beautiful now.-

The hills, covered in pine, came right down to the highway, and between the road and the sea were cliffs broken by the valleys of rivers with tiny estuary fans that glistened in the low tide. Jake couldn't see any houses, though they passed the occasional general store. It was all protected land, Karen explained, and there were no private dwellings permitted, except for a few homes that had been here for generations. Jeffers' tower would never be a tourist museum. You couldn't visit it unless you had the estate's permission. Camping wasn't encouraged on the beaches, some of which belonged to the home-owners.

-Up to the high tide line?-

-What?-

-The high tide line. At home, on the east and west coasts, the beaches are open territory between the water and the mark left by the high tide. Of course, if you get trapped, you can take the easy way out across someone's property. There've been incidents with irate landlords about that.-

-Well, you can't get to some of these beaches without going through an owner's gate. The surf and rocks are too rough, and there aren't any public trails to the cliffs and down. You'll see.-

After an hour they stopped at a small store and bought some fruit, cheese, bread, and cold ham. Leaning against the car in the June heat, as they shared a warm beer he still couldn't believe could be plucked from grocery shelves, she asked him about his love life.

Jake shrugged. -I don't know. It was pretty heavy for awhile. A woman, a little older than me and her friend, close friend. She had a temper, the woman, I mean. We fought a lot, and I turned to her friend for advice. It went on that way for a couple of months.-

-Did she find out?-

-Yes. We were breaking up anyway. And I told her because I felt guilty and angry.

-What happened?

-She slugged me. Not a slap, but a fist. It knocked me against the wall, and I came back charging. We pushed and yelled for a few minutes, and then it was over. I left or she left. That was in March. I haven't seen her since.-

-And the friend?-

That's more complicated, I guess. We kept sleeping together, on and off, until I came here. Nothing was resolved. I'm not in love with her, if that's what you mean.-

Karen looked at him, and her eyes were flecked with green light, the sun off the trees, he supposed. He felt confused. Sex went with the territory, didn't it? Sometimes soft and enjoyable, sometimes fierce and enervating, but always to be put away in sleep or other activity. If it had to do with love, he hadn't figured out the connection yet. Strong feelings, yes; call it passion if you like. What lay beyond he wasn't sure.

She laughed, and so did he. They were both nervous now, about where they were and what they were doing together. He wondered if they could *make* love. If that kind of exchange could measure their desire.

In the car above Cape Mendocino, Jake laughed again. He'd written about desire in what he thought were most of its guises, and much of that writing had been based on sexual relationships with women, usually brief ones, when moving on came quickly because of previous commitments on both sides. He'd once produced a whole verse cycle based on his three-day stay in the Laurentians with a Dutch travel agent he'd met in Montreal. She'd wanted to see some of wilderness Canada, so they went north to an isolated lodge recommended by a friend. The sky was enormous, and the lake a giant finger that stretched from north to south between granite cliffs. They fucked everywhere but in the cabin—in the woods, in sandy inlets, in the canoe by an island that kept disappearing into the mist. He said her name over and over until it became part of the landscape, like a tree or rock. When she had gone, he stayed behind and wrote in a fury he had never known before, as if to keep the name in place, as if he owned it and her and the lake he gazed at through the cabin window. The work won a literary journal prize, and he included it in a poetry collection a few years later. He sent the book to her at the

Amsterdam address she had given him, but heard nothing in reply. It wasn't the first time he had doubted his art.

A few more miles down the highway they came to a dirt sideroad that led off to the coast. A small hand-lettered sign said *Private*.

The road was very rough. It went right over exposed boulder tops and had potholes like mortar-shell craters after a battle. Halfway in they came to an old frame house that belonged in the backwoods of Georgia or Tennessee. Pots and other kitchen utensils hung from the porch eaves. Two giant water barrels leaned against the sagging ends of the house as if supporting it, and both were leaking slowly into the already saturated ground. Chickens wandered about, clucking, jerking their heads down at anything seed-like, and a large spotted rooster eyed them from a porch railing. Later, when he read James Dickey's novel *Deliverance*, with its weird hillbilly landscape on the edge of the wilderness, he would remember this place. But the old man who charged them a two-dollar toll seemed friendly enough, and asked them if they had been up to the music at Monterey. When they said yes, he cried out - *Somethin's happ'nin here; what it is ain't exactly clear-* and opened the wire gate on which another sign announced, *Beach, One Mile*.

The road was a little smoother now, but the trees arched over it, their branches brushing against the car body and the windshield, and the green light was everywhere. The car had a standard shift, and the engine raced when he shifted from first to second and back again. Then suddenly they were in the clear, as the dirt changed quickly to sand at the head of a small inlet. About a hundred yards away he could see the surf where some birds, gannets probably, dove cleanly into the white water and rose slowly in flapping display of wings and feather. Karen pointed to an eagle circling high above them.

-There's a Costanoan Indian expression I always remember when I'm here. *Noso'n.*-

-What's it mean?-

-*In breath as it is in spirit.*-

They rolled up the sleeping bags, put the food and wine in the knapsack, and walked single-file along the narrow trail. It was getting close to noon, and the sun beat on the backs of their necks. When she turned to smile at him once or twice, she squinted, and the small band of freckles on her left cheek danced in the glare. He watched her long-reddish brown hair swing across her shoulders, the outline of her legs and buttocks as her jeans tightened and released with each stride. He didn't know where they were going, but there was no hurry in either of them. He felt a tremendous tenderness for her, as if the fragility of their time together were its very strength, and a strange, bittersweet sadness, even as they grew closer, that would be the lasting impression for them both.

After Big Sur, Jake drove back to Toronto from California, courtesy of a car-hire firm, and enrolled part-time in the English graduate programme at the new university. His first course in Canadian literature was taught by a well-known writer who introduced him to Margaret Atwood in a Bay Street pub, gave him a major assignment on *The Stone Angel* (-Margaret Who?- he'd asked in each case), and showed him work by his city peers that challenged him to progress beyond the undergraduate submissions he'd made to campus magazines years before.

He began to write every day, verse and short prose pieces, and had a poem published in the college newspaper about a tiny Nevada town called Imlay with pictures of its two Vietnam war dead in the post-office window. The newspaper editor, pushing him for biographical information, found out that he had been at Monterey, and asked him if he'd like to write about the west coast sound that had taken over the pop world, not just the bubble-gum charts, but the new FM stations as well. So he tried to paint a picture of it all, Hendrix making it easy with "Purple Haze" at Number 1, and "White Rabbit" redefining wonderland for university students whose previous idea of *high* was a shared case of twenty-four on a Saturday night or, for the more supposedly more enlightened like himself, a few bottles of Beaujolais that Dylan had recommended in interviews.

There were various relationships. He picked up again with the friend of the woman who'd knocked him into the wall. They saw each other every week or two for a film or coffee, sometimes going back to her place for the night, sometimes not. They both seemed to prefer it that way, and occasionally she referred to a lawyer she had met, while he would mention come-ons from certain female students who had read his poetry. He did sleep with more than one of these young women, or rather they slept with him, letting him know when they left after a few days or a few weeks that the connection between them and the words he wrote was tenuous at best, and that, as with Cohen's currently popular Suzanne, he shouldn't confuse his body with their minds. One of them went on to become a feminist of national reputation, who led marches and wrote controversial pieces on gender issues for popular magazines as well as for academic journals. He met her at a party when his own fame was spreading, and she told him good-naturedly that his work was too much about himself and the gaze he levelled at his muse.

-At least you've read it.-

-Oh, yes- she answered cryptically. -I wouldn't have it any other way. -

He completed his M.A. and was able to teach a large American literature class from year to year at the university. His main income came from a book review column he did weekly for a major city newspaper, and soon his flat was wall-to-wall with first editions of Laurence, Bowering, Cohen, and the work of emerging writers like himself who published with the small presses that were burgeoning everywhere in the country. His first and then his second book came out to some acclaim, the poems passionate but carefully crafted according to the friendly critics, while others complained that the ardor was too controlled.

He stayed in contact with Karen, who finished up at Vassar and then worked in L.A. for a migrant workers aid group. She was part of the California protest about conditions for farm labourers, and fought the War as a state organizer until it was fought no more, and the million Vietnamese dead, and the 587,000 American ghosts and thousands of vets who began their suicides in the aftermath at home, cast a shadow she could no longer measure with her efforts.

...got a little sleep at 3 a.m. Pentagon concrete is not the softest bed. I'm not in jail, but can't think too straight. The direct action was a very frightening, very powerful, very moving thing. The military did not give us any sign of their intentions, and we were always unsure of what to do. There were several thousand people who stayed at least until midnight, and many beyond that, right on the Pentagon. We left about 1.00 a.m. when the cops started arresting our section piecemeal. If they had rushed or gassed us, we'd have stayed, but it seemed the point had been made, and all that was happening were more arrests and unnecessary violence at the front line. I'm supposed to write an article about it, but don't know if I can.

At first they exchanged letters fairly regularly, and shared their news, but it was awkward if he tried to phone. Either her boyfriend answered, or she was distracted in some particular way, and he found he couldn't explain his own love life anymore, or didn't want to. What he wanted to do was to cross the static space between them and return to Big Sur, this time to some kind of permanence he couldn't define and knew was impossible, based as it was on several unveiled hours in sleeping bags zipped together, a rock climbed in darkness, and a reckless leap in early morning light.

You know it all, I hope. There is nothing for me to say since you left. All of life seems to be playing in me, and all of it is you.

In the early seventies, when the war ended, she wrote she was getting married and going to Central America for awhile. He replied that she would always matter to him, and that they should keep in touch. It was their last exchange.

That afternoon they spent several hours walking on the beach, shoes left behind with the sleeping bags and knapsack, jeans rolled up to their knees. The white foam curled around their ankles and pulled gently at them, though beneath it the sand sloped treacherously away, and further out he could see the current rip where the waves broke on the rocks. If they slipped and fell they would slide all the way out to those rocks and never be able to fight their way back in. But they ran down the slope as the water receded thirty or forty feet, then turned, holding hands, to race ahead of it to the shoreline. It was the only hurried action of the afternoon. Held between the water and the hills behind them, hidden from the continent that stretched back to their other lives, they seemed suspended in time, as if this place were, without responsibility or regret, home.

What did she want to do after university? (travel). Would she ever visit Toronto? (of course). Did he ever think about teaching? That would take at least another degree, and he didn't know if he was up to that. He did want to go to England again; maybe she could meet him there, guardian-free. What did he like to drink? (scotch). What did she like to drink? (wine). Had she read *The Alexandria Quartet*? (no, but she would). Yes, she had read *Been Down So Long It Looks Like Up to Me*. Richard Farina was a cult figure on American campuses. Who was his favourite actress? (Julie Christie). Who was her favourite actor (Warren Beatty). -Maybe they'll do a film together- he said.

They talked a lot about the War, about several of Karen's high school classmates who were in Vietnam, and one older boy from Ferndale her sister had gone out with for a year who had died in the Ia Drang Valley in 1965. Jake hadn't heard of this battle, and she told him of the American unit called "the lost patrol" that had been cut off from its main group and surrounded by the enemy. It was the first large-scale encounter between the U.S. forces and the North Vietnamese Army. There was a lot of hand-to-hand fighting, and most of the Marines were wiped out. They should have seen the writing on the wall then.

-Do you have marches against the War in Canada?-

-Not really. More like vigils in front of the American consulate in Toronto. Sometimes eggs get thrown, and the police get called in. You have to realize we're known as the peaceable kingdom.-

-There's talk of a big protest march on Washington in the next couple of months. I hope it doesn't happen before I go back east. At that march in New York, a lot of guys burned their draft cards. They were arrested on the spot. But the student contingent was outnumbered or at least equalled by people of every other sort and age. The protest was amazingly universal. It's going to get ugly very soon, I think. Johnson's immoral. The whole damn thing is.- She turned away toward the water, blinking back tears. He didn't know what to say. No matter how much he cared, it wasn't his war, though the music he'd heard at Monterey could seem to make it so.

It got cooler and darker, and they went back to the edge of the inlet and built a fire. They made ham sandwiches without any butter and shared the cheese, swigging the wine from the bottle, getting high on it and the fresh air. A mist blew in, obscuring even the huge rock in front of them, and they zipped the bags together and got inside.

The Dylan song, the Bob Dylan song came to mind...*Just Like a Woman*...the lines rang through his head...could he remember the lines? *Nobody feels any pain*...that was how it started. Or was it? Could he remember the rest?

He'd started the song without thinking, as an instinctive reaction to the damp, and he knew she was listening, but the next lines came to him before he sang them. It would be a few years yet before he thought of this as one of Dylan's sillier efforts, but he wasn't sure now if he should go on.

-Bullshit artist- Karen said.

The rock, split off from the end of Cape Mendocino, startled him. He stopped the car and looked down. The tide was out, and there was a thin line of sand visible between the headland and the rock that towered nearly as high as the Cape itself. But the water had not receded entirely, and roiled around the base of the two opposing cliffs.

He drove slowly through hairpin turns to the shore.

How do you describe it, even when you were there, he thought. A boy and girl have sex on a beach, tangled in some sleeping bags. It must have been happening all over America at that very moment, *make love, not war,* so the extraordinary fused with the ordinary and became a number. Two became two thousand or two million, all the body parts dissolved into one another and the orgasm was collective, just what the establishment of the day expected of that dangerous group exchange, free love, soon to be commodified in video porn couplings and commune memories.

Jake realized that he had known very little about satisfying a woman in those days, very little about what she might prefer aside from delicate contact here and there, lips on a nipple, an ear; fingers irresponsible in their relentless, if gentle, motion downward, selfish extremities on a mission of lubrication only; and the inevitable plunge into that uncomplicated territory of pleasure, for him first and for her in auxiliary fashion, if at all. He had never felt inadequate or unprepared for his role, but as the mist vanished and the stars burned above them, he had failed himself before he could fail Karen.

As they kissed and struggled with their clothes, laughing at their snarled efforts within the confined space, he became afraid. He was older and supposedly wiser sexually, but nothing he knew or had done with others had much place here. The ache he felt within him wasn't about sex, and that he wanted to do things *for* her rather than *to* her

35

flooded his mind while his usually dependable organ flooded with nothing at all.

When they were naked he pressed against her, waiting for the reliable surge of what was meant to be some control over the situation, a predictability that could not be dissuaded or disbelieved. What happened was new to him, the casual circling of her fingers between his legs, as she spurred his tongued affirmation of her touch. The softness of her skin suprised him, and the way she pulled him to her, wrapping her legs around him tenderly but effectively, stroking his body to bring him slowly, certainly erect, without any feeling of urgency or preconceived plan of entry and dominion.

When he found himself inside her, he was drawn toward a vision of them held this way forever, borne on a mutual tide of generosity and assent. She came into him in ways that augmented and sweetened his own release. Although he searched for this experience in the intervening years, although he *wrote* about it, he never found it again.

They slept for several hours. When he woke the stars were brighter than before, and the sea was a sheen of black flecked with silver. The tide was coming in around the rock, but the water was very calm now, the surf farther out a susurrant feathering of sound he could barely hear. Karen stirred and lifted her head, brushing the hair from her face. She opened her eyes and smiled.

-What time is it?- she asked.

-I don't know. My watch is in the car. Must be two or three in the morning.-

-I'm hungry. Is there anything left?-

-No, I'm too tired.-

She slapped at him gently.

-Oh, food. Just a bit of bread and cheese.-

They ate it, and then shared an apple. The wine was gone, but the apple slaked their thirst a little.

-What'll we do now?- he said.

-Well, there is the obvious thing you mentioned. But you know what I'd like to do first?-

-What?-

-Climb the rock.-

-Are you kidding? There's at least ten feet of water out there, and it'll be freezing. And how will we see on the way up anyway?-

-It can't be more than fifty yards. Look how bright it is. I can see ledges from here.-

They got out of the bags and walked naked to the water's edge. The night breeze was warm on their skin. Karen went in up to her knees. -It's okay. We can make it.-

-Alright- he replied without much enthusiasm. -But we need to go across on our backs and hold up our jeans. I'm not climbing *that* without some protection.-

She laughed, came back, and kissed him. He curved into her as she pulled him down on the strand. If it was less astonishing now, it was no less intense, their mouths everywhere at once, their embraces so unique he wondered who had thought of hands before. This time there was no doubt, only the pleasure he was able to give to her in the space she gave to him. Afterwards he lay inside her, relaxed and unafraid.

-Women have the better view.-

-What do you mean?-

-You're looking at the stars. All I see are grains of sand.-

- *To see the world in a grain of sand.* Blake thought you had an advantage.-

-Look what happened to him.-

At Cape Mendocino, on the edge of the beach, Jake realized what he had wanted to say to her back then wasn't stupid, just not enough to meet the moment he had never been able to hold with words. Blake, he thought. *And eternity in an hour.* There was at least that much before the tide turned. He moved toward the rock.

-We can wear our sneakers. It won't matter if they're wet. At least they'll protect our feet.- She picked up her t-shirt and threw him his.

-They put on their underwear, rolled up their jeans, and waded backward into the sea. It was cold, and they kicked hard, leaving behind the relative light of the beach and moving into the shadow of the rock. The sneakers were heavy, and there was a bit of a current. Jake wondered if they would have to turn over and swim to avoid being carried sideways and around the corner of the rock. He felt something beneath the surface and yelled out.

-It's just a patch of kelp- Karen said. -Keep your arms and legs up or you'll get tangled.-

They came in against the black wall, grabbed hold with one hand, and shoved the jeans on a ledge. Then they clambered out, a thin, insulating film of water between their shirts and skin. It was awkward taking off the sneakers, pulling their jeans over wet legs, and getting their feet covered once more.

-Too much- he said, bending to tie his laces. -I think I'll swim back with everything on.-

-You'll wait a long time for the sun to dry your jeans. Not much fun driving when they're wet.-

-Yeah, okay. Meanwhile, let's see if we can get up here.-

The angle to the top was steeper than it had appeared from the beach, but the rock was igneous and scalloped with handholds. As they emerged from the shadow at the base, they could see a little better where they were going. What was startling, and what he had obviously underestimated, was the height of the rock. They climbed slowly but steadily for fifteen minutes, glancing down occasionally, and paying close attention to where they put their hands and feet. They were side by side, but did not speak, their breathing the only sound in the still air. Finally there was no more wall in front of them, only sky, and they scrambled onto a small platform at the top. The rock on its seaward side was u-shaped, and between the two projecting arms well over a hundred feet below they could make out a deep channel whose hollow, sucking sound suggested a large indentation or cave.

They shivered a little, but their shirts were almost dry. The stars were brilliant above them, and he lost count of what he thought were constellations. A satellite drifted overhead, the lack of depth in the blackness giving the impression of sidereal breakdown rather than technological proficiency. As it grew lighter they could see the kelp heads bobbing like seals in the channel, then several of the kelp heads barked and disappeared beneath the surface.

-Sea Lions- Karen told him.- They can't touch them here, but farther up and down the coast there's an annual cull because of the damage they do to nets and because the fishermen argue they're consuming the fish stock.-

-I'm sure they get into the nets, but how can they possibly eat up the fish?-

-Oh, one herd of several hundred will consume thousands of pounds of Pacific cod in a month.-

-On the other hand, what about the reproductive habits of all those cod who make it through dinner?-

-You should join the Sierra Club.-

When he turned to the perspective provided by the beach, he was shocked at how far they had climbed. Their clothes and sleeping bags were tiny pieces of driftwood on the otherwise virgin sand. The tide was at full height now, and the distance between the rock and the shore had almost doubled.

-We can always wait a few hours- he said.

-I'll be hungry by then. Besides, it's too rough for anything up here.- She ran her hand along a sharp line of summit stone, as if trying to smooth it out.

-Maybe we'd better go. I think it's going to take us a lot longer to get down.-

-She looked at him with mischief in her eyes. -Not necessarily.-

Their descent was much more difficult. Going up they had been able to lean into the wall, and Jake had searched for handholds only when his feet were securely in place. Now he had to hold on and let one foot at a time grope blindly for what seemed like razor-thin ledges. After twenty minutes they were only halfway down, breathing noisily, and getting tired fast.

Jesus- he said. -This is taking forever. My fingers and toes are beginning to cramp up.-

-Mine, too. Well, there is a solution.-

-What, jump?- he asked ironically.

-Yep. Are you ready for it?-

-Are you crazy? It must be fifty or sixty feet!-

-But the water's at least twenty feet deep now. Besides, I've done it before.-

-You have? From here? When?-

-When I was fifteen. We came on a school trip. My best friend and I got about halfway up and then lost our inspiration for the top. We were too tired to climb all the way back down.-

-So you just jumped?-

-Well, not quite like that. It took us a few minutes to find the courage. But then we made up our minds, held hands, yelled *Geronimo!*, and took off. It was incredible. Everybody who saw us cheered when we came up, but our teachers gave us hell.-

-I guess so. They would have had to pick up the pieces.-

-Are you going to hold my hand?-

He gave her a tight smile.- You don't think I'm going to jump alone, do you?-

They turned around slowly, taking shallow breaths, as intimate with the volcanic face as they had been with each

other, Jake suggested, when the manoeuvering was through.
-Is that what Simon and Garfunkel meant?-
He stared blankly at her.
-*I Am a Rock*.-
-*With my books and my poetry to protect me.*- He took
her hand and they stepped into space again.

It was incredible. He watched the sea rising up to meet
them, and for a brief instant took it all in—the sand, the
water, their t-shirts ballooning like tiny parachutes that
could not slow the rush. They stayed feet first, though from
any greater height they would have tumbled dangerously,
and hit cleanly, their hands breaking apart on impact, their
sneakers absorbing some of the shock. He was sure he
touched bottom, and when he opened his eyes underwater
he couldn't see her. He kicked hard, remembering the kelp,
and reached for the surface, breaking through with adrenalin
pumping and eyes stinging from the salt. She was there,
reaching for him with her strong hands, her hair slicked
back behind her ears, asking him over and over -Was it
intimate? Was it?-
-Bullshit artist- he shouted. -You never did that before.-

They were exhausted from it all—the night, the climb,
the leap—and gathered their belongings for the ride back
without saying very much. He held her for a long time
before they got in the car, rocking her gently as if to some
distant music. That afternoon he drove her to the airport
for her flight to L.A. They made no promises. There were
no definite plans. Maybe she would come to Toronto in

the fall. Maybe he would go to Vassar. They both expected something would work out, and were content to leave it at that. There would always be the letters. He didn't know the last one from Ferndale was the last one until it was too late.

→ *Today I couldn't read and went for a walk, feeling sick of people. I got down to the creek and meadow, and it was misting a little. I loved how it was, the trees and a strange air. I gave to it. But that couldn't be what one is striving for, not when the recipient is passive, to say the least. Yet what makes it so beautiful a sort of love is that it is so unselfish, and that I imagine is because there is no fear of rejection and therefore no need for dependency or possession. In other words, unselfish love can happen only when all selfish needs are taken care of. But to simply respond directly, emotionally, to people as one can to nature—there is a blindness to responsibility in that sort of state. You want an honest relationship—all right, what happens on the day when you are apart, and no surge of emotion carries you? Do you forget it until the next time you feel it, or is there a real obligation to keep love in mind, by force of will if necessary, without the security of which no one can ever quite give their entire self for fear of losing it to another?*

...I've always assumed that somehow we would both stay 'free,' maybe trapped-free and/or miserable, but a sub-cultural, familiar sort of free. Then, I think, even if that happens, how far apart our worlds will probably be...

After twenty years, Jake reached the base of the rock again.

II

IBIZA

A few months after Karen's final letter, Jake received a Canada Council grant and went to Europe. Toronto had become dull. Too many poets and too many parties where people read their latest masterpiece at the homes of older cultural figures of at least civic renown. These men gathered acolytes about them and held forth on a variety of topics from Canadian identity to the place of poetry in the modern world, but especially their own reputations. With few inhibitions at these get-togethers, a lot of nasty things were said about those who were absent or, if the host manipulated the mood, those who were in the crowd. When his second volume of poems appeared and received a strong review in a national magazine, it was the critic, not Jake, whom the literary disciples tore to shreds. Without a single reference to his book, indeed, while announcing loudly that they had not yet read it, they let him know that only certain kudos were worth having. He gave them no credence, but knew what they did not, that he was starting to repeat himself in his verse, writing more and more about local experience in increasingly fragile form.

The city was changing. No longer was the tallest building at the main intersection only three stories high. No longer was the Yonge Street strip an amazing combination of cadence and carnal, where you could hear Dizzy Gillespie,

Sonny Stitt, and B.B. King live, or move with semi-naked dancers to recorded pop rhythms by one-hit wonders. No longer did a cheap restaurant meal mean sitting in a high-backed booth, nursing a coffee for half an hour after you'd finished eating, and writing undisturbed while waitresses gave you room. And if you wanted more room, you couldn't quickly leave suburbia behind, despite the new expressways and viaducts. The surrounding countryside was owned by the very rich or by developers wanting to get rich. On his last trip to the cottage country that had once given the impression wilderness was nearby, Jake drove north for nearly twenty miles before he saw a large copse of trees.

He continued to teach his class and to write for the newspaper, but things were getting stale. The students weren't politically active or even politically aware after the War ended. They were happy to read on surface levels that weren't even there, and thought *Deliverance* was a simple tale about over-grown boys lost in the woods. When he introduced Atwood's *Surfacing* for consideration with the Dickey novel, the young men were bored, and the young women insulted that anyone would have to find herself by getting dirty and letting go of all the right words. As for his own reviewing, there were more books than he could handle, and too much good writing was getting left out. Although he'd been to several other provinces to read his own work, he hadn't been out of the country since returning from California.

The Canada Council grant was for $3000, a considerable amount of money in his part-time existence. He had some savings, and he struck a deal with the newspaper to provide a monthly thousand-word column from Europe. He gave up the teaching. Maybe one day he would get another degree; maybe not. He sublet his apartment, put his books in a friend's attic, and bought a plane ticket to Paris, with the intention of heading for Spain. A month before he left, and just before a reading in Kingston, he went to his high school reunion and met Sarah.

The small town where Jake had been a teenager was northeast of the city. It had grown too, in the intervening years, and was now a bedroom community for office commuters and their families. The fields he had roamed were covered with split-level houses, their double garages poised like predators to snatch unsuspecting, one-car couples. The dirt road he had biked to the local swimming hole was paved and widened to join with a major highway ten miles west. Traffic poured along this route, some exiting into the giant shopping mall that had replaced the horse farm stables he had cleaned out during summer breaks. There was a new technical school on the outskirts, but his old school was still standing in the town centre, the weathered *Boys* and *Girls* signs above entrances at opposite ends of the main building. The respective gyms were right inside each of these doorways; the girls' with a narrow running track anchored to the ceiling and walls ten feet above the floor, the boys' more modern with its six basketball nets and huge exhaust fans that sucked up bits of paper but never the stale smell of adolescent sweat.

He found the guys he had hung out with, their slicked-back ducktails now blow-dried into fashionable forms, their bodies beginning to sag in places from too much beer and too little exercise. They talked a lot about sports and cars, and offered him their business cards, decorated white rectangles that mentioned real estate, life insurance, and even the occasional law firm. When they asked what was up with him, he knew that his minor cultural reputation hadn't infiltrated their offices and board rooms, and when he said he was going to Europe to write, they made jokes about French and Scandinavian women. He imagined his own card, a red-fringed one that said *Poet/Gigolo— Rhymes Extra*, with a suitably down-and-out address.

Jake had never had a steady girlfriend at the school, but most of the older beauty queens were there, chicly dressed, their hair short like ebony or bronzed helmets without a hint of wear. They were all married, and all had kids, it seemed. Some had their husbands in tow, smiling men in Arnold Palmer shirts who looked annoyed or confused, or both, when introduced. And who could blame them? The reunion was about memories they didn't have, about sex before it was routine, about the way it used to be for someone else, not these packaged wives they thought they knew so well.

His teachers were more interested in what he had accomplished. They recalled his yearbook verses about northland wolves who were strong and free, or the very first poem he submitted about the Battle of Britain, whose constant end-rhymes justified the second part of his imagined business card: *Nine hundred British planes flew out/In the British pilot there was no doubt.* They hadn't read any of his recent work, but certainly would now, slapping him on the shoulder, saying he should come and talk to their students, encourage them to express themselves. Only the woodshop teacher he had hated was absent from the revelry. Apparently he had died of a heart attack a few years after giving out the lowest grade in all his years of instruction to the mangled tie-rack of a would-be poet.

On the second day, he saw Sarah in the girls' gym, where photos of championship teams and various pieces of athletic equipment were on display. He was leaning over the track railing, and she was standing beside a trampoline, the pride of the Senior Girls' Athletic Association when he had still to make a team, talking to another woman he also recognized. She looked up and smiled, waving to him as if he were an old friend. Jake lifted his arm in greeting, mindful that she had only tolerated his attentions back then. He had worshipped her unobtainable beauty and status, yearned for her with unrequited longing until she had left high school for university and he himself had little time for girls two grades beneath him. He went down to the gym floor, curious as to what they would say to one other.

She was shorter than he remembered, but still slim and obviously in shape. Her hair was dark and curly, unkempt by beauty pageant standards. He had watched Sarah through the chain-link fence around the tennis courts as she played with her boyfriend, or on the indoor volleyball court as she defended the net he tried in dreams to weave around her. He never spoke more than a few sentences to her after she had politely rejected his one request for a date, candid brown eyes already turning to other sights in front of the third-floor lockers. But she had remained aware of his loyalty for the next two years, and smiled at him when they passed in the halls or at assemblies in the auditorium. Although the smile always let him know, kindly but firmly, that she was beyond his reach, he never felt patronized by her.

It was another kind of distance now. There was a ring on her left hand, and after a few shared comments about the reunion, he discovered she was married and living in Montreal where she worked as a recreation director for the city. No kids yet, and her husband was a lawyer. He wasn't here.

-And you? I've read your books. I like some of the poems very much.-

The other woman's eyes glazed over, and she moved off after a somewhat graceless goodbye, promising to meet Sarah for lunch.

-Which ones?-

-The one about the boy who's lost his brother and fishes from your dock. The one about walking on the ice on Georgian Bay. Your outdoor imagery.-

-Thanks. You know, I always wanted to thank you.-

-For what?- She looked puzzled.

-For letting me down gently.-

-Oh, that. You were a nice kid, but two years in those days was a lifetime.- She added, as if by afterthought, looking across the gym at a group of noisy celebrants -I wasn't very happy then.-

-What do you mean?-

-I didn't know what I wanted to do with myself. I fought with my parents a lot.- Then she said something that really surprised Jake. -And I didn't like boys very much.-

He bit the *You could have fooled me* off his tongue. -Why not?-

-They were too pushy, always trying to go faster and further with you. Hormones. My urges were there, but slower.- She laughed. -I wanted a little more foreplay, I suppose.- When he raised his eyebrows, only partly in mock concern, she said quickly -I never actually slept with any of them. None of us did. Didn't you know that? Sure there were a few pregnancies, mostly in Grade Nine or Ten, and the girls were from much wealthier or poorer families than mine. Our class, didn't like taking chances, or didn't have to.-

Jake told her about Europe, and a little of why he was going.

-I know what you mean. But Montreal isn't Toronto. I guess that's why I stay.- It was an odd thing to say, as if there were no other commitments, and it was that sudden possibility that prompted him to tell her about his reading in Kingston in two weeks.

-It's on a Friday night.- He thought fast. -I was thinking about coming to Montreal the next day to see some friends. Maybe we could meet for lunch.-

She hesitated, though from coyness or real uncertainty he couldn't tell.

-I'd like that. But I'm not sure if I can. Here's my phone number at work. Call me from Kingston.-

Her plans for the rest of the day were set, and she was leaving on a late afternoon train, so they said goodbye.

-I hope I'll see you again- he said.

-I have a faded blue denim jacket that I wear.- It was one

of his own lines from a poem about California.

Jake spent a good part of the next twelve days making the rounds in Toronto, drinking too much, sleeping too little on couches in familiar apartments, and working on some poems about the reunion. There wasn't much point coming back after Kingston to repeat the dissolution trip, so he decided to pack what he needed, change his ticket, and fly out a week early from Montreal. A few friends took him to dinner on the last night, and then to a Stompin' Tom Connors concert. They hooted and hollered along with the big, happy crowd, and later had boozy exchanges at a Spadina tavern about the quality of Tom's songs. The consensus was that he was a genuine poet, mainly because that buzz-saw voice and banged up guitar, not to mention the boot itself, accompanied his lyrics.

-What did Stompin' Tom say when Paul Anka's girl-friend ran out of the room?- he shouted above the din.

-CAN, EH, DIANA!!- they yelled back.

The Kingston reading was at a small coffee house near the university. It could have been in Palo Alto. The walls were covered with large black and white posters of Bogart, Bergman, Bacall, Peter Lorre, and Edward G. Robinson, part of an ongoing festival for a mostly student audience. The sign in the window said the next film was *To Have and Have Not.* When he first saw *Casablanca,* Jake wanted to make love to the mature and luminous Ingrid Bergman in a whitewashed hotel room in which the curtains billowed gently in a sea wind, but the when nineteen-year-old Lauren

Bacall took an oral sex metaphor and filled it with experience and promise, he wanted to fuck her on a table in a seedy Martinique bar. He started to whistle as he stepped up on the tiny platform, turned with his books and sheaf of new poems in hand, and saw Sarah.

She was sitting at a table at the back of the room with a man who must have been her husband. He was clean-cut, but the denim shirt and leather vest looked out of place on a lawyer. R&R from the front lines, Jake supposed.

He read for about forty minutes, and finished with a funny poem about high school reunions and the failure of expectations there. Nobody, he said by way of introduction, can possibly live up to what they have become in your imagination. That was supposed to be it. He hadn't intended to read the one about Sarah once he saw her husband, but the wine he was sipping, and the knowledge he would get on a plane in twenty-four hours, broke through what were shallow impediments anyway.

-I did meet someone at the reunion who resisted my imagination, though. This is for her.-

It was about wet dreams and roads not taken and growing older. It was about the poet's inability to tell the dream lover when he meets her in the flesh that, despite his attempts to realize her, words cannot make up for lost years. An inability, of course, that Jake was attempting to deny by his very utterance on the page and in this room. *In dreams I dream/I touch then take you/The grade twelve girls can only stare/Their mouths awry.* Maybe Sarah would be offended or simply laugh it off; maybe her husband would find a way to translate it into legal language. He'd soon find out.

He signed a few books for audience members, and took his glass over to her table.

-This is Gary- she said.

-They shook hands, then Gary walked over to the bar for some more wine.

Sarah smiled. -He's my cousin. He drove down with me from Montreal. He's going on to Toronto tonight.

He looked at her left hand and the absent ring. -Where's your husband tonight?-

-I was divorced two years ago. I wore the ring to the reunion as a kind of protection. There's wasn't any time to tell you at the school, and I wasn't sure I wanted to.-

Gary came back and placed a bottle of burgundy on the table between them. He kissed Sarah on the cheek. -I'm off- he said. -He looked at Jake. -Thanks for the reading.- A plain leather vest, Jake noticed, as Gary disappeared into the crowd. No beads.

-I guess we should ask what this is all about.-

-It goes back a long way.-

-For me it does, but I was the one who had a crush on you, remember?-

-Yes, I do. But you've become important to me in the past couple of years. I picked up your first book when things were going downhill in my marriage. What you said about men and women was very romantic, but made sense sometimes. There was a back cover photo, so I knew what you looked like. I wanted to see you again, but didn't know if you'd come to the reunion. You always seemed such a loner in high school. Why did you go back?-

-Professional curiosity.- He caught her smile. -No, really. There were things I'd left behind there, and I wanted to see if I could write about them.-

-Such as?-

-Such as who we all were before things started to explode. There's a gap between us then and who we've become.-

-So you try to cover it with words?-

-Some of it. You heard part of the effort tonight.-

-Am I a gap?-

-You have been. Maybe you still are.-

-I think you hide behind words.- Her voice was strong, stronger than he had expected.

It was strange in the hotel room, strange when they took off their clothes and got into bed. Before tonight they had spoken for five minutes in a dozen years, and before that they had never spent any time together, only passed in crowded hallways as she eluded though never completely evaded his desire. They weren't teenagers anymore, and any romance was in the contrivance of the poems that had partly brought them here. But they were both eager for sex, and what they did with their bodies without metaphor was full of knowledge and possibility.

When Jake woke in the early morning he was curved into Sarah's back, his arms around her. He thought of making her laugh by doing a Bogart imitation and telling her that where he was going she couldn't follow, but he knew this would be an attempt at private escape. Movies were one thing, but there were the very real limitations of their common frame or two of experience, and the scripts of their intervening lives.

She had to get back to Montreal by noon. There was a girls' soccer tournament that began at one o'clock. -That's why I couldn't have lunch with you today- she told him.

-I'm flying out from Dorval at midnight. We can have a late dinner.-

They drove straight to her apartment where she changed into a track suit. She kissed him when she left, gave him a spare key, and said she'd be back by seven.

Jake spent the afternoon up on the mountain, watching the city, and thinking about the coming year. It would be fall soon, and though it wouldn't be so cold by the Mediterranean as here, he wanted to be settled in somewhere before the rains became constant. He had no plans other than to read and write. He was taking a few paperbacks, and would purchase more at an English-language bookstore in Paris. As for his writing, he had his typewriter, and he wanted to try something larger and more ambitious than usual. He looked over the drop-off to some rocks at the foot of the mountain and the duck pond there. *Mont Royal.* Just a big hill. It couldn't be more than fifty or sixty feet. He thought of Karen. The blue waters below were shining like the sea.

Sarah was waiting when he got back to her place at six-thirty. One team had failed to show, so they had a round-robin elimination and then a championship game.

-Who won?-

-Rocco's Pizza.-

-Let's help Rocco celebrate. What's the number?-

After they had demolished the pizza no movie scripts came to mind. The fluid lines of their bodies needed no rehearsal. He felt very comfortable with her, but knew if he stayed any longer he might not go at all, at least not for awhile, and then it would be harder to leave. It was the part of him that wanted to stay who spoke.

-Sarah, do you want to come over to Europe sometime in the next year?-

-Where will you be?-

-Spain, and then probably Greece. Could you get away. Do you want to get away?-

-Getaway.- Her conjugation was intentional. -What about you?-

The Cape Mendocino rock was huge. Jake wondered how much of it lay beneath the sand. Not like an iceberg surely, although it seemed to be floating in the air. Where was the centre of a rock's gravity, and how much erosion at the base would there have to be before it rolled over in the waves? Well, his weight wasn't going to make any difference. He rubbed his hands with wet sand, touched the face for the first time, and began to climb.

Jake spent only three days in Paris, staying at a hotel with a circular, tower-like staircase in Montparnasse. He visited the Rue Cardinal Lemoine and the little square where Hemingway wrote some of the vignettes for the first edition of *in our time*, and he climbed an older winding staircase to the top of Notre Dame. That was enough height for him this visit. The Eiffel Tower would have to wait. He had *café au lait* and *croissantes* for breakfast at sidewalk tables, and wondered, in his self-absorption, whether all the women of France dressed and walked like the Parisian women who made their trip to the office seem like a stroll to an early-morning assignation. By the Seine he watched the hawkers with their wares on push-wagons and the painters with their palettes and berets who painted the bridges much as their counterparts must have done centuries before. At Versailles, there were a lot of tourists jabbering away in German, Swedish and English, the latter bent in loud, declarative terms into various American shapes. There was nothing like a Boston burr or southern drawl in the Hall of Mirrors to remind you of the rise and fall of empires.

On the third night he boarded the train for Barcelona, having decided between Stompin' Tom songs to take the advice of a friend and try the Balearic Islands, Formentera in particular. Lots of cheap farmhouses and great beaches. He asked the porter when they would cross the border, and requested a wake-up call. At dawn, the train edged between the Pyrenees and the sea, and pulled into the Spanish town of Port Bou. Men dressed in frayed black suits marched up and down the platform, thrusting clouded bottles of *gazoza* at eager hands stretched from the grimy, half-open windows. Women in voluminous black dresses, more regal in demeanour, sat behind stalls of fruit and flowers, waiting for the trade to come to them. This was the passport control of northeastern Spain, and along with all the others Jake disembarked, carrying his large knapsack and heavy typewriter. The border guards with their silly tricorne hats and very serious manner were opening everything. A mixture of stockings, shirts, and children's clothing hung from suitcase lids or was strewn over counters.

They stopped him because of the typewriter. *Journaliste?* one asked, while another slowly spelled out the Smith Corona letters stamped on the case.

-No, I'm a writer.- Like Lorca, he wanted to say, but knew better. On the wall behind the guards, the unsmiling portrait of *El Caudillo*, the Generalissimo, gazed down in disapproval at any possible remnant of the International Brigade.

-And what do you write?- asked a third man who suddenly appeared. His English was perfect, and he wore a handgun at the waist of his neatly-pressed khaki pants.

-Poems.-

-What kind of poems?-

-Love poems.- Jake left a trace of question in his reply, as he sought the approval of Franco's dangerous minion.

-The man laughed. -*Un hombre del amor!*- he shouted lustily to his companions, and banged hard on the typewriter cover. -Make sure it is nothing more than that, *amigo*.- His voice again smooth and controlled, his obsidian eyes replete with warning.

Jake changed from his *wagon-lit*, purchased only for the night, to an added third-class coach filled with amiable Catalonians and small cages of nervous chickens. As the train moved toward Barcelona, it passed through stands of birch and tall pines, and he saw, for the first time, the Mediterranean light that flooded down on the grass or brown needles of the forest floor. The air between the branches and the earth seemed luminous, the copses like church interiors carved from wood and light, and the train like a moving pew in which he sat in votive homage.

The churches were pillaged by the entrance to the city. Mile after mile of shacks, shabby and denuded in the sun, the riven faces in the doors and windows staring back at him from histories he could not begin to understand. These dwellings were gradually replaced by apartment blocks whose older inhabitants were invisible, and by concrete school grounds where children stood in placid groups as if in eternal recess from the world.

He took a cab to the port from the station, and purchased a ticket on an overnight ferry to Ibiza. From there he would take a smaller boat across the five-mile channel to Formentera. There was nothing much to do for the rest of the day, but walk the *Ramblas*, the medianed main street with its shops and cafes, and listen to the soft *th* sound of the Catalan language as it replaced the *c* and *z* of the official tongue: Bar*th*elona, *cerve*tha, *gra*th*ias*. The central bull ring was closed, but he was able to visit the matadors' museum and gain some sense of death in the afternoon from the photographs of Joselito, Belmonte, and more recently, El Cordobes, whose movie star looks and unorthodox genius had divided the Spanish public and changed the style of bullfighting, if not the rules, forever. Those who were feeling brave could walk out along the tops of the narrow walls above the paddocks of the bulls whose bulk surprised him, and whose horn tips clicked relentlessly against the stone beneath his feet.

The ferry ride was uneventful, and when he came on deck in the morning the coast of Ibiza was only a mile away. The hills were high and pine-covered, and fell down to the sea where waves rolled onto sand like uneven white lines in a grade-school drawing. The air was warm, though the sun was not yet high in the sky, and the vividness of the blue and green colours of the water and island was startling. He made a mental note to get some sunglasses before the next boat ride.

The old town of Ibiza was set on a hill above the harbour. All the buildings were white and of the Spanish *finca* style, with the cathedral at their very top, its bell-tower battered and eroded by the wind, but borne up by the firm alliance between church and state that had been Franco's certitude for almost forty years. The harbour stirred with activity, fishermen and market people mingling with tourists, other Ibi*th*icans rushing to and fro, engaged in commercial activity of one kind or another. The small boat for Formentera was leaving almost immediately, and Jake had time only to buy the ticket and have some coffee and cake on the quay.

There was a colourful canopy stretched across the open deck that offered passengers protection from the sun, and rows of fixed deck chairs, like theatre seats, facing the bow. The channel between the islands was choppy, but the air was so clear and invigorating that he did not feel queasy. Gulls followed them from shore to shore, screeching as they dove for bits of bread tossed overboard by a crew member.

At the Formentera jetty he boarded a bus to the inland capital. Once the road rose to a plateau above the sea, the landscape was flat and dusty, and virtually treeless. Cactus hedges grew alongside white adobe walls behind which sat farmhouses in isolated disrepair. The street of the capital village, not town, had been dug up for some pipe-laying. A bulldozer that looked like the construction equivalent of a Model-T sat in the main square caked with clay, while tourists sat in chilly groups in the verandah shade of the hotel, facing the Spaniards across the way who chatted beneath the woven cane extension of a café roof. Jake went inside and ordered a *portocolado* and some *fritos*. To the left of his table was an ancient pinball machine with a portrait of Betty Grable etched in the glass. A cluster of Spanish kids was watching a tall German or Scandinavian manipulate the thin line between replay and tilt. Jake ate slowly, somewhat concerned about what he had found. It seemed wholly alien to what he had imagined, and not very conducive to creativity, more like a movie set gone to seed than another country he had yet to discover.

His hotel room was surprisingly modern, with new bedding, a shiny *bidet,* and louvered wooden doors that led to a balcony overlooking a pool. He went for a swim after checking in. The pool was only thirty feet long, and the salt water stung his eyes, but after several lengths he felt refreshed. He had a shower, then fell asleep and dreamt about trees.

That night he approached the café owner about farm houses for rent. The man spoke fairly good English. -Yes, very cheap- he said, and pointed back along the road from the port.

-Any others?-

-Oh yes, but to the north and far from here. You would need a car or motorcycle.-

-How far?-

-Ten miles, maybe more. Used to be a village up there. Not now. Very lonely for you, I think.- The man grabbed his own crotch for emphasis. -You know?- he said.

The next morning Jake rented a motorcycle and went north without much optimism. The landscape here was more of the same. There was no shade along the road, and he had to drive very slowly because of the rocks upthrust through the dirt. It took him well over an hour to find the first house, set back from the road and facing the sea. The view was spectacular because of the sea, and because the green hills of Ibiza were directly across the channel. He stared at the hills for a long time after he had checked out the dilapidated interior of the building, furnished with a table and chair, a bed with slats missing beneath the thin mattress, and some plates and cups beside a one-burner hotplate.

-You find it?- the cafe owner asked when he returned.

-Yes and no.-

-Cómo que, si o no?-

Jake caught the boat back to Ibiza the same afternoon.

In a restaurant near the harbour he met an American writer who had lived on Ibiza for nearly thirty years. His first novel, with a vaguely familiar title, had come out at the same time as *The Naked and the Dead*, and the reviews, according to this writer, had been better than Mailer's. He'd been working on a second novel for a while now, but it would be done soon, and then he would go back to New York for the celebrations.

-What you want- he said complacently -is Avila. Some interesting ex-pats, and great houses available in the hills not too far away.

-Why aren't you there- Jake asked politely. If his underlying irony was audible, the American didn't notice.

-Was there. Ruled the roost for a long time. Now I need the big city lights for inspiration.- He spread his arms, taking in all the buildings and people majestically.

Avila was about twelve miles from Ibiza town and on the same side of the island. The main street was paved and lined with plane trees. The trees grew randomly in the square at one end of the street where he was eventually to meet expatriates knocking back brandies or cold *cervezas* for hours, talking about art.

North of the town was a river valley, surrounded by high hills, and it was here, after some direction from local farmers, Jake met Elly and her husband, Americans who had hitchhiked around Europe in the fifties and settled on

Ibiza at the time he had started high school. They had a large house and a small, furnished *finca* for rent on a corner of their land. He walked across the walled fields with Elly, a striking woman with high cheekbones and long, black hair who spoke Spanish fluently. Not an exile, he thought, but a *conquistadore* descendant repossessing her homeland.

-How long do you think you'll stay?-

-For the winter, at least.-

-Are you a writer?-

-Yes. How did you know?-

-Everyone here's a writer- she said. -Every *man*- she added.

-Your husband?-

-Oh, he's an exception. He sells houses to writers.-

-What about you?-

-I weave. Wall hangings, rugs, *serapes*.-

-Do you sell your work?-

-Sometimes. In Avila. The mayor owns a rug.-

-That should make you feel secure.-

-No. If the police chief had one, I'd feel secure.-

The house was small, but clean and well-furnished. There were three rooms. In the central one across from the thick, wooden door were an open-hearth fireplace, a table and bench, and a cushioned chair that would be comfortable for reading. A propane lamp was suspended by a chain from the ceiling; its solid cylindrical tank dangled ominously by his forehead.

-You'll have to watch that- she said.

There was a two-burner hotplate with its own propane bottle, and a pile of dishes beside it. A screened-in cupboard hung from the end of a rope beside the stove.

-Ants get into everything if you're not careful. Sugar and meat especially. If you have honey or jam, you'd better put the jar in a dish of water, even inside the cupboard.-

In the bedroom were a double bed covered with a colourful wool blanket and a big cardboard box.

-Those are books the previous tenant left behind. You're welcome to them.-

He opened the box. It was a godsend. He hadn't been to the Paris bookstore, and had only half a dozen paperbacks in his knapsack. Here were at least fifty more Penguin, Panther, and Faber & Faber editions. Mostly fiction from the look of things. Orwell, Dashiell Hammet, Virginia Woolf, Robert Graves. His winter's reading was set.

The third room was a storage area, complete with bucket for indoor plumbing needs on cold rainy nights. Otherwise, there was the cactus patch beside the house.

-I'd like to live here. How much is it?-

-Fifteen hundred *pesetas* a month.- As he struggled with the math, she told him. -About fifty American dollars.-

They shook hands.

The house was five miles from town, so Jake bought a motorbike, an old BSA Firebird that looked and sounded as if it had been over every dirt trail in Europe. He rode across the valley and up into the hills where the wood man lived, and a few days later a battered truck dropped off his winter's fuel supply, gnarled logs and pieces of unidentifiable stump mixed with occasional smooth softwood boards, remnants from a sawmill or carpenter's shop. It was all dry from the summer heat, and would burn well. There was a lean-to at the end of the house near the well, where he stacked as much as he could before putting the rest in the storage room.

The days were hot, and he rose early to work in the mornings, sitting at the table with the door open and the flyscreen shifting slightly in the breeze. At first he concentrated on the newspaper column, writing about his time in Paris and the trip down to Spain, trying to get it right for jaded Toronto readers for whom Europe, along with yesterday's paper, was ancient history. He sent postcards to various people, including Sarah, pictures of the island in touched-up colours that made it seem like a tropical paradise, telling them *South Pacific* had been filmed in a tiny village on the north coast, Mario Lanza singing to those Spanish extras deemed most likely to pass as Polynesian.

He bought ready-fry steaks and pieces of scrawny chicken from the main-street butcher, and plenty of fruit from the outdoor stalls. The evenings were long, and he didn't need to light the propane lamp if he went to bed without reading. After supper he would sit outside on the low stone wall with a coffee, and look at the pine-covered hills where he had been told there were traces of Phoenecian forts and ancient threshing floors. Once or twice a week he would ride into town after his meal and have a coffee and brandy in the main-square café, chatting to some of the English and American writers. Several of them had been on the island for more than a decade, working on their novels that no one, it became clear, was ever meant to see. One of them made an annual pilgrimmage to an isolated *finca* up in the hills where he apparently swore off booze and drugs and wrote all day. Only for two weeks, he said, as most of his book had to reflect his real life here below. All of the writers knew the Mailer clone and partied with him on a regular basis in Ibiza town.

It was the painters who impressed Jake. They not only got their hands dirty, but sold their work in galleries in Barcelona and Valencia, and elsewhere in Europe. He found this out even though they didn't like to talk too much about what they did themselves, but spoke instead of those whose work they admired, which they went to see in the Prado in Madrid and in other galleries whenever they could. Paintings by a few of them hung in a waterfront café in Avila, abstract-expressionist figures and Mediterranean landscapes that pushed constantly against the frame. They had an artists' jazz band, and played free-form material on Friday nights in the same cafe, the benzedrine and beer breaking down the chromatic scale into tiny, pulsating parts and reassembling them in new and inordinate ways that made him listen like never before.

He became friends with Russell, a Blackfoot from Montana, who played the tenor sax and wore a paint-splattered black t-shirt, rain or shine, though sometimes it was covered with a fringed buckskin jacket that remained impeccably clean.

-My father, who, unlike me, could paddle a canoe, gave me this when I went off to art college. He said he could accept my being a painter in the white man's world, but if I ever came home with any stains on it he'd take a brush to me. My father had a good eye. I didn't want to inspire him.-

-Is he still alive?-

-Nope. He died watching the tv broadcasts from Wounded Knee. The longer the siege went on, the sicker he got. It broke his heart, the split between the band leaders and the traditionals, the guns he hated but knew were necessary. He'd been active in the late fifties with the group that eventually became AIM. He tried to talk to me about it, but I was long gone by then into art and the urban life. Taverns where you were known because of what you did, and even if they called you 'Chief' they couldn't keep the respect out of their voices.- Russell grimaced slightly, and looked off at the sea. -That's what I told myself then.-

-When was the last time you were home?-

-Montana? For the old man's funeral. I sold a couple of big ones to carry me there and back. The thing is, I would rather have shown them to him. I played sax at the ceremony. An *un*traditional I guess they called me.-

-Jazz Band stuff?-

-Are you kidding? No, a ballad that I'd heard Archie Shepp do, called *Going Home*. Drop by the house sometime, and you can hear it. The guys in the band would disbar me. All puns intended.-

Another time he asked Russell why he'd come to the island.

-Ah, some people in New York kept going on about the *light*, how I'd never see things the same way again. They might have mentioned something about booze and women too. They were right about those. I keep looking for the light. I've glimpsed it a few times. Why are you here?-

Jake told him about Toronto and the way it had closed

in on anything creative. About how he thought he needed space to write something more—*other*— than poems. No, he hadn't started anything yet, and he wasn't going to talk about it when he did, at least not to anyone who wasn't Spanish.

Russell laughed, and waved his arm in the direction of some expatriates at another cafe table. -I know what you mean. Those guys are Tolstoys when it comes to conversation, but I'm not sure what's being put down in the notebooks.- He doodled a self-portrait on the back of a paper coaster and held it up. -Other than *that*, I mean.-

In late October it got much colder at night, and the rains began. Jake purchased a thick wool poncho to keep him warm on the bike. It served the purpose, but felt like chain-mail on his shoulders when it got wet. Twice on the way back from town in a midday downpour, the wicker bag of groceries looped over the speedometer and resting on the gas tank between his legs, he turned too quickly from the paved road into the morass of the dirt track. Beneath the mud there were ruts twisting into more ruts in serpentine confusion, and the tires couldn't hold a line. He flipped off into the red mire, almost suffocating beneath the pancho, the food spread out for yards, the bike contorted but undamaged beside him. At the *finca* he stripped down and hung everything by the fire, but only when the sun broke through in the afternoon did the pancho dry, and then it was stiff with mud that he had to beat out with a stick rather than take a chance on shrinking it in the big wooden tub where he did his laundry.

Because of the rains he would buy enough food for two or three days, stopping for his coffee and brandy at noon since it was too dark and cold to return to town after supper and ride home later on. He would go in for the Friday jazz bash and stay over at Russell's, but he was learning to get used to the lonely days and nights, as he threw lots of wood on the fire and opened the box of paperbacks, moving steadily through *Homage to Catalonia, I Claudius,* and *To the Lighthouse*, Woolf especially burning into him as Lily Briscoe tried to find the right form and colour. It was her search that initially turned him toward his own work, the finished poems tiny reflections of his daily existence, the possibilities of fiction gigantic in comparison, bulldozing their way over the quotidian, demanding time that he had to give but was not used to giving up.

He wrote to Sarah soon after he sent the postcard, but there was no reply. Maybe it was because he had not mentioned her coming over, and did not describe his Ibizan life in much detail, talking instead of Franco's politics and the habits of the exiles. He felt close to her from a distance, but was not yet ready to apportion a territory he had only partially explored. At some point, he was fairly sure, he would want to see her again, but why should she wait around for him until then, especially in Montreal where, unlike Toronto, the breath of romance was rarely soured by sexual expression?

Right now, it was Elly who enamoured him. In her early forties, she was fifteen years his senior. Her facial features reminded Jake of Baez, though the husky tones of her speaking voice suggested an altogether different kind of singer, if she sang at all. She wore peasant blouses and long skirts when he saw her in town, and was always going somewhere when he tried to engage her in any extended conversation. After a couple of polite refusals to join him for coffee, it was clear that, while friendly, she wasn't interested in his company, a fact that only made her more attractive as she waved to him from her Renault van on the road into town, or smiled when they met at the post office and asked courteously about the *finca* or his work.

-Stay away from that one, man- Russell told him. -She's trouble.

-Trouble? Sounds like you're talking about some horny young thing after an older guy.-

-She's horny alright. And she's already found the older guy.-

-The husband? I've only met him once.-

-Not him. The movie mogul.-

-You mean Penumbra? White linen suit and long gray hair.-

-None other.-

Richard Penumbra had been on Ibiza longer than anyone could remember. He was English or American, or both, his mid-Atlantic accent carefully protecting rather than revealing any origins. Where his money came from or was laundered remained a mystery, though he was lavish with its distribution to Avila nightspots. He had produced several Hollywood films of dubious quality back in the fifties, including one with a very young Tuesday Weld. Now he was reported to be the behind-the-scenes financier of spaghetti westerns made in Spain for Italian and eastern European consumption. He drove a Jaguar, the only one on the island, and held extravagant parties at his villa by the sea, near a beach called *Figuerales*.

-Well, I guess my true romance is over. I can't compete with Gatsby.-

-And she ain't Daisy Buchanan, believe me.-

-Does everybody know about this, Elly and Penumbra?-

-Everybody but her old man, it seems. And I think he knows, somewhere deep down, anyway.-

-*How long has this been going on?* Cole Porter said that.-

-Or Noel Coward. All those guys sound the same. The rhythm never changes. Three or four years I'd say. He has other ladies when he flies off to Madrid and Rome, but Elly seems to be his main squeeze here.-

-And she's happy with that?-

-Must be. You could always ask her.-

He didn't, of course, not even when she stopped by the *finca* one morning to invite him for supper at her house.

-Gordon wants to meet you. We're having some friends in. Do you like *paella*? Good, how about Saturday night? Oh- she added, without a trace of irony -it's casual dress.-

He borrowed Russell's buckskin jacket, and discovered that it did smell slightly of paint.

-You look like a real Indian. I'm proud of you.-

-Thanks Chief. And I do respect your work.-

-What is it they say in war? Keep a tight asshole.-

-Meaning?-

-Just don't say anything you don't want to say. And try not to act surprised.-

-What do you know here that I don't know?-

-Let's just say you're a third party, and I've been a third

party on occasion.-

Jake walked along the top of the walls across the fields to her house. It was dusk, and the swallows were flitting back and forth among the trees. The wind blew in from the sea on the other side of the hills, and he could taste the salt in the air. That afternoon he had started a poem about Elly, looking for ways to make her less elusive, and then found himself in a prose passage about Karen or someone like Karen who hadn't met him yet and was growing up in Ferndale, California. He was still puzzling over this creative connection when he knocked on the door.

It was Gordon, tall and florid-faced, who answered and shook his hand. -Welcome- he said. -Come in and meet some friends of ours.-

At one end of the large dining room with its wooden beams and colourful wall hangings was a semi-circle of chairs in front of a stone hearth. He heard Elly's laughter and saw the white linen suit. Maybe it's a lined winter version, he thought spitefully. Sphincter clenched, he joined the company.

Richard Penumbra looked through him when they were introduced, sniffed slightly as if he had an allergy to buckskin, and turned back to his conversation with Elly. On his other side was a much younger woman in a shiny, sheath dress who didn't know what casual meant. But since she was quite attractive and immediately began to ask him about why he had come to Ibiza, Jake tried to ignore her satin display. He told her a little about himself, and learned that she was from Naples and here just for the weekend, at Richard's invitation. She was due to appear in *Los Cabelleros y La Senorita* which was to begin shooting in the coming week in the Sierra de Guadarama near Madrid.

-That's where *For Whom the Bell Tolls* was set.-

-I don't know that one. Who was in in it?-

-Gary Cooper and Ingrid Bergman. The earth moved.-

-Oh, I like disaster films.-

There was another couple from Ibiza town, a contractor and his wife, who talked animatedly with Gordon about tearing down old *fincas* to their shells and rebuilding them with all the modern conveniences for tourist use between April and October. There was also a young Danish architect who worked for Gordon, and who turned the actress's head at the supper table, talking to her about film opportunities in Copenhagen, though Sergio Leone remakes weren't what he had in mind. This left Jake at one end of the table with Penumbra and Elly who didn't make too much effort to disguise their affection for each other, employing him as a useful decoy from time to time, as they ate their way through the salad and *paella* courses. Jake was furious at Elly because he was so attracted to her himself, and fascinated by the way she seemed drawn to Penumbra's flame.

The movie producer had a pallid face and a stocky body that didn't promise much in bed for a lithe and healthy woman who was at least ten years younger, though maybe sexual prowess couldn't be measured in decades or flesh tones. He also had an acerbic tongue that threw off barbs like rabbit punches to kidneys you couldn't always protect. After a few comments to Jake about Spanish wine and the history of Avila to which he obviously did not anticipate any learned response, Penumbra said -Elly tells me you write. What is it you write, exactly?-

He looked at Elly, trying to decipher his place in their private conversation, but her face was blank.

-Poetry.- It was a naked and unprotected word. He imagined the architect fucking the actress on a Copenhagen sound stage.

-Ah, but what kind of poetry, dear fellow? No, let me guess. From your jacket I'd say you were a pure romantic, writing lyrics to lost maidenhead and short verses about your lonely situation here on the island. Am I right?-

The disdainful accuracy of the assessment stung him, but before he could respond, Penumbra touched his sleeve. -Haven't I seen this before?-

Never mind your asshole, Jake thought, watch your jugular. -You're right, Richard. I have a Tuesday Weld fixation and use pasta to clean my guns.-

If he expected Penumbra to choke on his wine and turn beet red with anger or embarrassment, he was disappointed.

-You see, Elly, our young man is romantic. Can we do anything to alleviate his loneliness? Unfortunately, Maria is off to Madrid tomorrow.- He nodded towards the actress who, hearing him mention her name, smiled brilliantly in their direction. -But the evening is young. Perhaps she could persuade you to reveal some of the- Penumbra paused for the effect -tools of your trade.-

Jake stood up. -Thanks for the meal- he said. -And yes, you've seen this jacket before. It belongs to a friend of mine. An Indian, actually, who knows more about the American

West than you'll find in any Spanish imitations.-

It was a lie, of course, at least in terms of Penumbra's western lore. Russell would rather ride a decaled Harley than a dappled horse into battle, and talked more about the history of jazz than high noon discord.

He apologized to Gordon at the door.

-Don't even think about it, Jake. It's better that way.-

-You said that to him.-

-Yeah, just a bit of third-party rhetoric.

-That I know all that cowboy and Indian stuff?-

-Of course. You're the resident expert now.-

-Hey, I've got a reputation to protect.-

They were drinking beer, sitting in Russell's studio that ran the whole upper-floor length of his house on the edge of town. There was paint everywhere, as if his t-shirt were only a palette he brought with him to the café. Charcoal drawings of women's figures in various positions were pinned to one wall, and photographs of what must have been the original naked women in similar poses. Leaning against the same wall were oiled reds, blues and greens fused together in expressionist array. The sun pouring in the windows was just another colour. On an old wooden easel was a newly-stretched piece of canvas waiting for the brush.

-I thought you made it all up out of your head.-

-I do. How do you think I get to take the pictures in the first place? And what about you, Robert Jordan? You turned down Maria. What about your inventions?-

He had returned to the *finca* after the exchange with

Penumbra, uncorked some red wine, and stirred the fire. He picked up a book, read a few lines, and put it back on the table. Then he sat before the Smith-Corona and began to write. She was eleven years old, and out on Cape Mendocino with her parents. They found a dead female seal washed up on the beach, its body scored with abrasions.

-Rogue male- said her father. -Too much weight in mating.

She wanted to bury it, but her mother said no, it was better to let the gulls have it, and the crabs. Later she told this story in front of her class as a nature report. When she had finished, her teacher said -Thank you, Karen, you may sit down.-

For awhile he didn't know where he was going with this. He was still calling her Karen for one thing, when it was clear he was in new terrain without any experiential guides. But the words began to take care of themselves, finding their place on the page before he willed them there. By the time the sun rose, and he had killed the bottle, the words were deep into Ferndale in the mid-sixties, approaching a point when he might have to face himself in fiction.

-I can't really talk about it now. It's kind of complicated.-
-Okay. As long as you know what to do when the time comes.-
-What time?-
-When Penumbra rings your bell.-
-I can't see him doing that.-
-He'll send her.-

For two weeks Jake stayed incommunicado. He went

into town every third day for supplies, breaking his work rules by doing so very early in the morning, arriving as soon as the stores and street stalls opened at seven o'clock, and returning to the *finca* where he would write well into the evening, as he did on the days when there was no need to leave home. It all unfolded: the girl's high school years; the death of her father in a car accident; her boyfriend who joined the army in '65 and went off to Vietnam the year before she left for college in the east; his decision to re-enlist, thus ending their relationship-by-correspondence; her journey to London with her mother and aunt where she met a Canadian university student, slightly older, who wanted to be a writer.

Then it stopped, the creative flow that deluged his days with something more than memory, because it was behind memory, and allowed him to distil his fiction through his time with Karen. He imagined that she had told him these things about her childhood and adolescence, that he had walked the streets of Ferndale with her, and that the dead-seal beach was three hundred miles up the coast from Big Sur. But he knew all along he was reinventing her, writing her absence into his version of her existence, when contrivance alone took him further and further from what he had to admit was her unimagined *presence* in his life. Where he would go from here depended on who she was now, even for a moment. He would have to find that out.

He had long forgotten her Ferndale address, where perhaps her family still lived, but surely it was available through telephone information. He could have asked Russell to help him with the technical Spanish, but this was something he didn't want to share. It was too fragile, too bound up in what he was trying to pursue on and off the page. Russell would have understood, but all the talking would have taken the edge away, what he thought to be the sharp line of distinction between himself and those expatriates who wrote in circles or conversed endlessly about their material, as if white space could be filled simply by words.

So he stood in the post-office booth, babbling to a Catalan operator whose ancestors might have seen the California coast from three-masters that sailed around the Horn, or built the praesidio at Monterey before James Cook shouted England's name for all the empirical world to hear. But either he couldn't get her to comprehend his request for overseas information, or she was telling him that he had to deposit *mucho pesetas* that he didn't have in his pocket, or it just wasn't meant to be. Frustrated and about to hang up, he heard a tapping on the booth door, and turned to see Elly smiling at him through the glass.

Jake found himself explaining to her his need to get through to the States and obtain a number, sensing his tone of voice and maybe his expression were giving away more than he intended. But Elly spoke calmly into the phone, using the information he provided, and after a minute or two he was connected to a woman with the familiar California twang who put him on to the Ferndale exchange. The result was anti-climactic. Karen's parents no longer lived in Ferndale or the surrounding area. He even tried the San Francisco region, but the operator said there were over fifty persons listed with that surname.

-Can I buy you a coffee?- she said, as they stepped out

of the post-office together.

-Yeah, sure. I mean, okay, thanks.- Karen was on his mind, and what to do next. They walked over to the main square, scuffing with their shoes the dusty leaves that had fallen from the plane trees, and sat at a table in the shade. Jake was at a loss, sipping his coffee, half-listening to Elly saying something about Penumbra, when he thought of Vassar. Of course! He could write to the Registrar's Office, or better still, the Alumni Office that kept track of famous former students like Jackie Kennedy. Surely he could find an address.

-...a few people on Saturday night, nothing fancy. Would you like to come?-

-What? Sorry, I was thinking about something else. Would I like to come?-

-To Richard's. Saturday night.-

-Why?-

-Why not?-

-Come on, Elly. You sat there for our discussion. Why should I bother? Why should *he* bother?-

-He likes you. You've got *cajones*. Something not too many men display in front of him. Besides, he's got a proposition for you.-

-What kind of proposition?-

-He wants to ask your advice about a screenplay. Maybe get you to make a few suggestions or emendations.-

-A screenplay? I'm sure he's got dozens of minions to do that for him. Why me?-

-It's about Byron. You're a poet. And I've told you, you've got balls.-

-And *I'm* supposed to be the romantic.-

-You are, Jake. That's the other thing in your favour.

-What about you? What's in your favour?-

Her face tightened. -It's not something I talk about.-

-Okay, Elly, let's be up front with one another. You're involved with this guy, fine. How Gordon deals with it is none of my business. But just because I'm attracted to you as well doesn't mean you should be a shill for Penumbra and ask me to do something he should ask me himself.-

He could see she was very angry, but he was angry too, knowing he was turning down an offer about Byron that, although tainted on the personal level, in creative terms was very enticing. Before she could speak he said -Look, I don't like Richard Penumbra or how he uses people. I *am* a poet, which means I won't make any money from my writing, not screenplay money anyway, but for better or worse I write because I have to, not because anyone else pays me. It wouldn't work.-

He would never forget what she told him as she stood up to leave, her black hair blowing in the breeze, her dark eyes fixing him with an intensity he couldn't avoid, and didn't want to deny. Despite her anger, her voice was not harsh, and in his envy of Penumbra's apparent possession of her, he was unsure as to whether she had thrown him accolade or imprecation.

-You're through- she said.

-Just as well- Russell told him. -You might have become rich and famous, and what would that have done to your art?-

-Byron, for fuck's sake. I think it's an autobiographical screenplay he wants to produce.-

-Yeah, probably. Who could he get to play the great man? The Duke's too old. Redford's too pretty. I know! Dennis Hopper. Byron comes in on a Harley with Lady-what's-her-name sitting side-saddle, and recites *Hells' Angel*, an ode to joy.-

-Maybe you should let him know you're available.-

-Maybe I will, but that's not going to get you anywhere with Elly.-

-I'm not going anywhere with Elly.-

He'd sent the letter off to Vassar, asking for Karen's address. He wanted to keep writing about her, but sooner or later Big Sur would be involved, and he needed her permission to approach that storied landscape.

-She's not finished yet- Russell said.

It was cold at night, and Jake usually fell asleep in front of the fire, his legs stretched out on the hearth, the book he had been reading resting on his chest. He woke at two or three in the morning, turned off the lamp, and made his way to bed. If his pancho was dry he used it for extra warmth; if not, he wore a sweater beneath the blankets, and with the tiny window shuttered, lay open-eyed in a dark so profound there was no difference when he finally shut his eyes from fatigue. In the mornings, the well-water was often murky from the soil that had been washed in by the rain, and did not completely clear even after an hour's settling in the bucket. The hills were obscured by veils of rain, and he waited for the promised almond blossoms and perfumed air of spring.

He set aside the Karen pages and wrote newspaper pieces about such things as the benefits of a cactus patch in lieu of indoor plumbing and the joy of cooking on a two-burner hotplate. He extolled the fresh-baked bread that only cost a few *pesetas,* and the smoky *jerez* that took the chill away after a motorcycle ride. The wood pile diminished, as did the heap of unread books. In two overcast days he went through Hammett's *Red Harvest,* Kozinki's *The Painted Bird,* and a Spanish exile's graphic account of the bombing of Guernica, translated into English as *The Day the Sky Fell Down.*

One afternoon, when the sun was out, he rode north to the town where *South Pacific* had been filmed in the mid-fifties. Subsequently, he told his readers of the tattered Mitzi Gaynor poster that clung to a *taverna* wall, and how one of the palm trees that had been imported for the movie set had been preserved in the town square and appeared to be flourishing. Another time he went into Ibiza town and visited the cathedral, the carved wooden font and stained-glass panoply providing more than enough for commentary, along with his report of the black-cassocked priest who talked softly to him about *los bravos,* not the members of the International Brigades but the *fascisti* who had died in the island's prison during the Civil War.

He also wrote some poems, including an ironic one about Elly who spread her inspiration among too many would-be poets, with silence the inevitable result. He didn't see her except from a distance in town, and always left the rent money at Gordon's tiny office near the police station.

Penumbra, of course, did not approach him, though more than once the Jaguar passed sleekly as he stopped the bike at one of the crossroad corners leading into the main street. After awhile, the lost opportunities with the screenplay, and with Elly, faded away, and he began to consider where he would go after Spain.

It was February. The pink and white almond blossoms were on the trees behind the *finca*, and the rose bush bloomed beside the well. Sheep and goats from neighbouring farms nibbled at fresh tufts of grass in the surrounding fields, and left neat black droppings where they grazed. Jake put aside the pancho and rode every day into town in shorts and a light sweatshirt, his legs turning slightly pink, then brown, from the wind and sun. The first busloads of tourists began to arrive in Avila, filling the main square with chatter and exhaust. It was no longer so pleasant to sit and read a newspaper for an hour while sipping a *leché caliente* and dipping bread into the spilled liquid in the saucer. People came up to him because of his blond hair and blue eyes and tried to engage him in conversation about Sweden or Germany, undeterred by his lack of knowledge about Malmo or Cologne. He and Russell formed a club of two. Membership was restricted to those North Americans who could no longer speak English. When a tourist approached for information or companionship, Russell would start yelling in Native tongue and Jake would respond loudly in pig Latin or by reciting Lewis Carroll's *Jabberwocky*.

-What the hell's a 'slithy tove'?-

-It was a chant used by the Crow to celebrate victory

over the Blackfoot.-

-Uh-huh.-

The letter, when it came, was not the awaited one from Vassar. It was postmarked Montreal, and as he opened it he recalled his invitation to Sarah to come to Europe. She was writing to tell him she had arranged several months away from work, and was taking a holiday in London at the beginning of April. She was sorry she hadn't been in touch sooner, but she'd been trying to deal with some feelings about her ex-husband, and by the time they'd been resolved she didn't know if his proposal about Europe still stood. Did he want to see her? She had enough money to pay her own way, wherever they went.

His response was mixed. He'd had no sex since leaving Canada, apart from lonely releases beneath blankets and the pancho while Elly spread more than inspiration in his dreams. He valued the connection to Sarah that drew them both back into the past, and formed the basis of so much of their attraction to one another. But he had spent only one night and part of a day with her. Was there more to talk about, enough to sustain a relationship or even to begin one? There was also Karen in his life, a deeper past, and what he needed from her to go on with his writing. In the end, he decided that celibacy wasn't a groundrule for creative expression. If Karen was a presence, she was also a muse he couldn't bed, while Sarah was a vital figure in the flesh whose immediacy might temper the isolation in which he had worked for the last seven months. He wrote to tell her they could meet in London in mid-April, and asked her how she felt about going to Greece.

Jake thought he had settled things with the island. Russell he would miss. The ragged edges of their exchanges after too much beer, the music they listened to in his studio and talked about at cafe tables, the perceptive responses to his poetry, and the opportunity for him to watch an artist at work, the way in which Russell stretched colours and made light a form you could see *and* touch when the paint was dry but not the vision. They spoke about him coming to Greece, but both knew it was unlikely.

-Have brush will travel, eh?-

-Something like that. Can't you guys do it anywhere? On stones or walls by the side of the road?-

-The head of a pin, the Sistine Chapel. Nothing to it.-

-But seriously, man. A different island, different women. There won't be as many tourists, I'll bet.-

-Those goddamn buses will disappear come September. And what do you think, the women here don't come and go? Besides, I've got my business career to think about.-

-What are you talking about?-

-Didn't I tell you? Penumbra's commissioned me to do a portrait of him.-

They both started laughing, and smacked their fists on the table so hard the pigeons nearby got nervous and flapped away.

-It's Dorian Gray- Jake shouted. You'll have to do a copy and keep it in the attic.-

-Yeah, right. With a little Picasso and Miro thrown in. When what he really wants is Andrew Wyeth.-

-Or Winslow Homer. Do him in the linen suit in a rocking chair.- They were rolling now.

-I could put him on a soup can. Nude, with a Rubens body. That's worth five grand.-

-Five grand?-

-Yep. That's what he offered. He came to the studio last week. 'Russell,' he said, 'I've been thinking I'd like a self-portrait done.' 'That's one you do yourself,' I almost replied. But then he asked, 'Would five thousand American be sufficient?' After I had picked up the broken beer bottle that had metaphorically slipped from my hand, I figured my bargaining days were over. So I answered calmly, as if I got offers like this all the time, 'That'll do.' He's coming by tomorrow for his first sitting. Jesus, I hope I can take it all seriously.-

-Think of the art.-

-Yeah, here's to art.-

They raised their glasses. -And to big bucks!- they shouted. The pigeons eyed them warily from a distance.

The day before Elly crossed all the borders she herself had created, the Spanish farmer who kept the sheep and goats in the nearby fields told Jake a story about two dogs in the neighbourhood who were determined to be joined despite some strong efforts to keep them apart. The bitch, who was in heat, was kept indoors because she had already produced two litters of pups in the last year, and was let outside, under close watch, for only a few minutes at a time. The male, much larger, hovered around the *finca*, enduring sharp stones and execrations hurled at him, and even beatings with a stick if he came too close. Once, he got up on the roof via a wood pile and began to dig away at the chimney. Jake imagined leaning over the hearth and looking up to see the tenacious canine etched furiously against the sky. The bitch started to moan, so the farmer went out with a shotgun aimed high, but the male escaped before any damage was done.

Then one morning, without thinking, the farmer opened his door and unzipped to take a leak. The bitch was between his legs before he could stop pissing, and the male was on her in the courtyard in a matter of seconds. They were humping away joyously when the farmer stumbled toward them, struggling with his pants. The male turned, trying to dismount and run simultaneously, and the result was the two of them got stuck together ass to ass. The enraged Spaniard grabbed each of them by the scruff of the neck and yanked them apart. Both howled, though whether from *coitus interruptus* rather than actual disengagment Jake wasn't sure. Now the bitch had a full litter in her stomach, and the male hadn't been back.

-*Bastias!*,- the farmer said disparagingly, and spat in the dust. -*Qué se puede hacer?*-

He was sitting at his usual café table, reading the *International Herald-Tribune*. There was a review of a new novel about Vietnam coming home to California; Nixon was still resisting Watergate investigators; and the Amazon rain forest was being overrun by gold miners. He recalled a short story in his high school English anthology, "Leininghen Versus the Ants," in which a wealthy Brazilian plantation owner risks all to save his economic empire from tiny but innumerable invaders. Hollywood made a film of the story, "The Naked Jungle," with giant Charlton Heston firebombing the pincered hordes when mere squashing would no longer do the job. Her shadow fell across the newspaper just as Leininghen-Heston watched the wind shift to save the plantation from flames. Not so long ago, Jake would have asked his class to figure out her symbolic import. Now no one made him more aware of the critical spaces between art and life.

-The car is in the garage. Gordon will get it later. Can I get a ride home with you?-

-What about the Jaguar- he almost said. -Sure. Do you want to go now, or can I finally buy you a coffee?-

She laughed. One eye tooth looked like a pincer. No, he told his class, too obvious.

-Let me buy you a coffee- she said.

He told her about the gold miners in the Amazon, though not about Leininghen.

-It reminds me of Ibiza. Not so long ago, two or three dozen people passed through Avila in the summer. You could go down to *Figuerales* and swim nude.-

You and the Rubens body, Jake thought. -Did you?-

-Did I what?-

-Swim nude.-

-All the time.- Then she surprised him. -Do you want to?-

-Do I want to what?-

She smiled and sipped her coffee.

-What, now?-

-Yes, now.-

-Won't it be cold?- She must be testing him. A Penumbra script.

-A little. But the sun will keep us warm.-

Where was Russell when he needed him. A little levity, the painter's eye. Anything would help. Elly, he wanted to say, do you want to fuck me, or does Penumbra want you to fuck me? Then he remembered he was leaving in two weeks.

-Okay- he said.

Jake wound up the Firebird on the curved road through the pine forest before the pavement dropped on the other side of the hills to the sea. There were moments they hit eighty on the short straights, her arms tight around his waist, her breasts soft against his back. The smell of the pines was strong, and the oleander was in bloom along the rim of the road, the blurred scent of the plant mingling with that of the trees. The beach was empty, and there was a gentle surf on the rocks, the blue and white breaking over the tanned edges of Elly's body in the clear light as she stepped out of her shorts, took off her blouse, and moved toward the water. He shucked off his clothes and caught up with her as she ran into the sea, his mind's eye filled with a sun-shaped mole on her thigh, the ribbed sand beneath his feet, and finally with the sudden shock of entry as they plunged together into the waves.

-Don't go out too far- she told him when they surfaced, the salt stinging his eyes. -The current won't let you back in.-

They swam parallel to the beach, a few metres apart, then rolled over and floated, gazing up at the enormous sky. A cerulean bowl turned upside down, sculpted so long ago it no longer mattered whose fingers brushed the clay or what sea-gods or goddesses surrendered in reply.

He didn't know how or when to make a move with her. He didn't even know what to say. If Penumbra had walked along the beach and sat down by their clothes, it would have at least untied his tongue. Maybe she would fuck them both then, and the pleasure she took would replace the price the producer would have him pay. But no white-suited figure strolled into view. The line of sand was distinctly uninhabited beyond her closed eyes, her black hair floating around her head like an aura or perhaps Medusa's curls. What would his class do with such symbolism run amok?

She opened her eyes, turned on her stomach, and paddled over to him. -What are you thinking- she asked. Then they were on their backs again, holding hands, kicking themselves offshore, moving east along the route Phoenicians had plied. The blood coursed through his legs. The thin layer of water on his chest was warmed by the sun, and his face was dry with salt. He stopped trying to come up with an answer to her question. He didn't think, felt only a nascent connection to her, the sea their common mother, as they were borne together by the current and their own incipient rhythms. After a long time, they turned in a slow circle and headed back to the beach. Nearer the strand they let go, and she swam away.

Jake stayed where he was, treading water, and watched her emerge from the sea. Her back arched toward him, she reached over her shoulders and wrung the water from her hair. Then she bent over, hands on her knees, and began to swing her head from side to side, water dripping from her buttocks to the sand, her hair wheeling in the bright light, the space between her legs a still point in the universe around which he could revolve forever.

But she would not accept his homage. By the time he got to shore she was in her shorts and blouse, tiny drops of sweat on her upper lip as if she had hurried. He dressed self-consciously beside her, as she sat and gazed at the sea, the sand drifting from her fingers when she lifted it gently and let it fall. When he was done, she stood up and brushed his salt-rimmed hair with her fingers before walking toward the bike.

-Elly- he called after her. -What was it all about?

-It was what we had- she replied. Then she turned and looked at him. -Fucking isn't everything.- She was smiling, but she looked sad. -You think it is, and that without it, you haven't been the distance. I've swum nude here before, and I've fucked a lot on this beach. But I haven't done what we've just done with anyone else. I won't forget it. I hope you won't either.-

They rode home slowly, her hands on the metal bar behind her, his thoughts on what she had said, and on what he was trying to write about Karen. Two different women and two different beaches in time. How would they come together on the page?

-So you're writing with a hard-on now. I know the feeling. The pen in the hand is worth two in the bush. Or something like that.-

-Yeah, only the Smith-Corona makes the metaphor a

bit unwieldy.-

-It's her nude portrait I'd like to do, you know. Do you think she'd pay me?-

-Maybe you should ask Penumbra.-

-Can I use you as a reference?-

-Feel free.-

The day before he left, Russell unrolled an oil painting in the square. In it Jake was sitting at the cafe table with a pen in his hand, gazing up at a plane tree figure with something like Elly's face, if you knew Elly's face, and the marvellous, curvaceous lines he had seen so many times in Russell's work, not very much like Elly's body, if you knew Elly's body. Russell was at the table too, his hands waving, obviously talking a blue streak, his long pony tail extending brush-like from his head and pointing suggestively upward at the figure.

-I call it *Conversation*. You can call it what you want. Hang it on your wall in Greece.-

-You just took a wild guess at everything but the face?-

-Hey, artists take chances. Besides, it's all symbolic anyway. Isn't that what you've been telling me?-

They hugged one another. Jake knew he wouldn't see the painter again. He wouldn't come back to Ibiza, and Russell wasn't likely to leave, except for short trips to the mainland. They respected one another, maybe they even loved one another, but there wasn't much to say.

-I'll send you a postcard.-

-Take it easy, man. And remember, I can read as well as paint. So send the writing too.-

-I will. Maybe some stuff that will surprise you.-
-You're an open book.- Russell said.

He sold the bike to a Spanish kid and gave him the pancho as well. It was too heavy to carry, and besides, it belonged to the island. He hoped Elly would come by as he packed up his few belongings, to check on the *finca* and say goodbye, but she kept her distance, and when he shook Gordon's hand at the office in town he didn't ask about her. Penumbra was invisible, almost as if he had never existed, a fantastic Mephistophelian who tempted and discarded equally, his allure based on perverted Faustian cravings for money and fame. Was Elly the Helen figure? No, if Penumbra had sent her, she would have fucked him ragged and there would have been a subsequent demand on his mind if not his soul.

He looked for her in Avila, as he waited for the bus, but by the time he was at the port in Ibiza town and had boarded the ship for Barcelona, he was already turning toward the other end of the Mediterranean. He realized he would be meeting Sarah in two weeks, and there was much to sort out. He leaned over the railing by the bow, and surveyed the harbour buildings whitewashed in the sun. Somewhere down there was the Mailer clone, welcoming yet another callow writer with stories of the naked and the dead. And down there was that slightly younger version of himself seeking a way on. Then as the boat slipped away from the quay he thought he saw her, in the same shorts and blouse she had discarded at the beach, standing by a white Jaguar, her arm raised in farewell or shielding her face against the light.

Jake waved and started to shout to her, but his voice was taken by the wind.

III

MYTHOS

When he got to the top of the rock, his jeans were torn at the knees, and his thighs were trembling. Jake smiled. After he made his way down, he wouldn't have anything left for sleeping-bag exchanges, and since the Pacific tide was out, he couldn't shorten the trip with a jump. Besides, even at high tide, he was almost fifty; the shock of hitting the water would probably kill him.

*

As Sarah walked through the arrivals door at Heathrow, he didn't recognize her. It wasn't only because her hair was below her shoulders, or that she walked in the straightforward North American way he had almost forgotten, all her body language announcing she was ready to embrace or take on the world, whichever came first. It was because he was looking at that once-familiar image of himself he had left behind in Montreal when the past was barely dry on the page and he pursued and slept with it because it reflected his desire.

She came up to him and kissed him on the cheek. -*Hola*- she said. *Cómo estás?-*

Jake hugged her and ran his fingers across her back, pressing her close, this old-new woman who, he realized suddenly, would make demands on him that he had not even tried to anticipate. On the train north from Barcelona to Paris, and then on the ferry from Calais to Southend, he had thought about Ibiza, about what he was leaving behind and why, and about how much he wanted to see Greece and start again. He had read Layton and Cohen, the *isolomanes*, or lovers of islands, who wrote poems about the Aegean archipelago with an intense, self-centered passion that nonetheless celebrated the people and the milieu while lamenting the invasion of barbarians like themselves. Though Jake knew Lawrence Durrell's lush, ironic portraits of Corfu and Rhodes were decades gone, there was still the rumour you could take a boat to an island, and then a smaller boat to a smaller island where tourists did not exist, and fishermen sipped *ouzo* at marble-topped tables or smashed plates on the floor and danced their refusal of the Colonels' regime.

In London for a week, he had holed up at a small, Earl's Court hotel, dreaming of the Big Sur landscape, treading water in a sea that would kill him if he did anything other than swim fast to shore, watching a naked Karen bend over a table where Russell sat painting on the chipped enamel surface, while on a watchtower above the dunes Robinson Jeffers dressed as Hendrix sang the electric question: *Is it tomorrow or the end of time?* In the mornings, when he tried to sort the dream out on paper, the words resisted and the images stayed surreal. The day before he went to meet Sarah at the airport, he checked out of the hotel and found a bed-and-breakfast near Hampstead Heath. He had already booked them an open ticket flight to Athens, which he made sure was refundable because now she was close he wasn't sure how it was going to work out generally, let alone in detail.

-Tell me about Ibiza- she said, as they walked on the Heath that afternoon. -You didn't say much in your letter.- From the airport they had gone straight to the bed-and-breakfast and a pliant mattress that sank in the middle, preventing escape. In his initial nervousness, Jake forgot what they had previously accomplished as lovers, and wondered if their time together in Kingston and Montreal had been just the brief recovery of high-school infatuation that should have released their adolescent hormones and set them free. Sarah was tired from the plane ride, and he couldn't recall the rules or move easily to the absence of rules with someone he hardly knew. But sexual appetite took over, and in their mutual need they climaxed without delay, the pillows absorbing his muffled indications of other names had she been able to translate the text he was in.

-Its hard to explain. I'm still trying to absorb it. Maybe write about it. I'll try to tell you, but not yet, okay? You and I have to start now. I don't want to know about your ex-husband and how close you came to going back to him. I don't want to talk about the past anymore.-

-Jake...- She tried to speak, but he kept going. -We came together last fall because of high school and the reunion, but we need to find out why we're together now. Whatever has happened to us both since then we still want to be here. Let's take the next few months and see what happens.-

It was more than he had wanted to say, and certainly

more of a commitment than he had expected to provide, but he was not unhappy with his effort. He was here with her whatever the complications of Ibiza, whatever the space he needed to write about Karen and that other past he could speak of only to himself. As for Sarah's space and experience, given what he was prepared to relinquish, she would surely adapt.

Athens was hot and confusing. Spanish had been fairly easy to pick up, many of the words similar to French, and there were all the old westerns he could cull for such terms as *adios, buenas dias,* and even *vayan con Dios,* which was what Mexican peasants always told the American gunfighters who were moving on. But Greek was a puzzle. For one thing, the alphabet was completely different, and gave no clue as to how individual letters should be pronounced. When he looked at billboards or road signs, Jake had no idea what they were saying, unless numbers were involved. The taxi driver on the way in from the airport chatted away as if they understood, however, and dropped them with some elaborate explanation in Omonia Square, pointing at ornate facades of buildings that suggested entrances to hotels.

They chose an unpretentious foyer on a side street just off the square, and were given a top floor room, its large balcony festooned with flowers and facing south, so the afternoon and evening sun did not shine directly in. The view was of other roof-tops and more television aerials per capita than in London or Paris. When they tried their own set, the choice was between a home-town soap opera and

M*A*S*H with Greek subtitles. Hawkeye's version of another country was preferable to the unscreened world around them.

There were many cafés in the vicinity, and they ate their breakfasts of fresh-baked bread, yogurt, and strong Greek coffee—*metreo*, they learned to say, 'with a little sugar'—at round metal tables with wire-backed chairs, their menus with inked-in English terms beside the references to Hellenic fare. For their lunches and suppers they went to the *Plaka*, the old city beneath the Acropolis, where servings were generous and cheap, and *bouzouki* music pounded through speakers into the street, the sound mixing with that of unmuffled delivery trucks that roared through the narrow confines of the district.

Everywhere there were hanging banners that said **April 21, 1967**, the date the Colonels had taken over the government. The machine-gun soldiers in abundance at the airport had been the first indicators that politics here were operating at a much more fragile and dangerous level than in Spain, though there didn't seem to be any immediate signs of war, and certainly no discouragement of foreign visitors. In contrast to his Spanish entry, no official tried to crack the Smith-Corona code, but Jake knew the Greek army officers enforced their power through the terrible practice of the *falangia*—beating the soles of the feet with an iron bar or leather strap. He was more aware than he had been in Spain of contributing to the economy of dictators, but rationalized it was better for the vast majority of Greeks who opposed the regime to interact with those who would employ such terms as *demokratia* and *elevtheria* ('freedom,' according to the *Herald-Tribune*) in different fashion from the frightening men in uniform.

They learned that gatherings of more than a few citizens were banned, as was the traditional smashing of crockery in restaurants or taverns in celebration of anything at all, and read the *Herald-Tribune* reports of hostility between Greece and Turkey over boundary lines between the eastern Aegean islands and the Turkish shoreline. Things were especially tense on Cyprus where an activist Turkish minority was augmenting the decades-old division about *enosis* or union with the mainland.

One afternoon, they went up to the Acropolis. They avoided the guided tour and wandered randomly through the site, overwhelmed by history despite the recent sandblasting and refurbishing of columns and temple roofs. They sat in the top row of the restored two thousand-seat amphitheatre where the plays of Aristophanes and Sophocles had been performed, and then walked on the stage itself, quoting bits of *Hamlet* and *Macbeth* from high-school memory when *Timon of Athens* would have been more appropriate. There were signs in different languages forbidding the removal of any material from the grounds, but Jake picked up some pieces of stone from the base of the main building and slipped them into his pocket. Whether they were two and a half millenia old or droppings from the restoration, he couldn't tell. He knew if he were caught the distinction wouldn't matter, and wondered at the punishment involved. Were foreigners merely fined and deported for stealing the past, or were they turned over to the peodiatrists of the present Greek drama?

He chose Lesbos because of Sappho, nothing else. He had read a collection of her lyric fragments, and gathered from its introduction that she had lived in the village of Erossos and then in Mytilene, the capital. He had no special desire to follow her home; the general ambience of her birthplace would do. It was the third-largest island in the Aegean, in the northeast corner of the sea, beneath the bulge of Turkey where ancient Troy had fallen. Like Ibiza, much of it was covered in pines.

They took an overnight boat from Piraeus, going deck-class because the tickets cost next-to-nothing and because the idea of sitting up much of the night beneath the constellations and waking in the early morning as the ship approached their storied destination overcame their need for comfort or privacy. After only an hour or two on board they were adopted by a group of Lesbos truckers returning from a delivery of olive oil to various mainland distributors. These men spoke some English and plied them with pasta and retsina, while softly singing songs they denied were those of Theodrakis. They put their fingers to their lips when Jake mentioned the composer's name, and said, *siga, siga, pedi mou*, which, he found out afterwards, meant 'go slowly, little one.' The result was no sleep, and a bleary dawn at Chios, thirty miles south of Lesbos, with a range of treeless brown hills not far behind the semi-deserted quay.

Mytilene, a few hours later, was very different. The port surged with traffic, and the hills hovered over the buildings with green display, coming right down to the water's edge on the outskirts of town. There was a statue of Sappho in the middle of the curved road that ran behind the sea-wall, the plaque on its base revealing nothing but her name in Greek and English letters. An old fortress, called the *Castro* on the map Jake had purchased, dominated the skyline above the harbour. They sat at a café with some *metreo* and studied the map. Erossos was, in fact, tempting, but located west of the capital in a dry, volcanic area of the island. He wanted to get as far as possible from whatever tourists came here, and needed some guidance until he found brief descriptions of villages on the map's back side.

-Listen to this- he said to Sarah. -*Mythos is a charming village approximately forty miles from Mytilene. It is built on the side of a mountain above the sea and boasts a 13th-century Genoese castle with wonderful olive groves beneath.* From the topographical colouring, the map says there's more trees than rocks.-

-Let's try it. We can always come back here and start again if we don't want to stay. Besides, maybe Sappho went there for dirty weekends.-

-I'm feeling inspired already.-

-You could do some writing, too.- The inflection on the adverb was barely discernable.

Their love-making since London had been frequent and not at all self-conscious. They felt comfortable with one another in bed, but not so familiar as to deny explorations and discoveries that gave new pleasure. Despite his admonition on the Heath, Jake still wondered what had brought them to this naked give-and-take so many years after she had been the elusive older girl who had haunted his fugitive dreams. He had known nothing about her then, except the imagined curve of her body beneath tight sweaters and skirts, nothing about what she thought and felt, and in Montreal there had been no time to move beyond their sexual exchange to find out what made her tick. It was evident, though, from her brief high school references, that she had not imagined anything about him when they were young. So the chance she had taken by coming to Europe, based on his poetry and their fleeting physical contact, seemed more vital than any risk of his own.

In London they had traded paperbacks, he giving her a volume of Lorca's poems, some of which she already knew, and she offering him Lessing's *The Golden Notebook*, which he was reading and enjoying. They talked a lot of politics and culture—the still-open wound of the FLQ Crisis and the quality of *Québecois* rock lyrics, among other things—and when they disagreed had heated debates that usually ended with one of them making the other laugh through some imitative gesture and breaking off the contest. They both had a sense of fair play, and an awareness of their own aggressive tendencies under fire, so while they often came at the world from different directions, their view of various arrival points was not so incompatible or exclusive.

He liked the way she stood up and danced with the truckers on the boat as the juke box blared, her movements open and relaxed, her smile friendly when she met the eyes of the men, her eyes smiling when she looked at him. She had begun to open doors through the warmth of her interactions with others, and teach him that her independence at such times could include her feelings for him. He felt as he followed her lithe passage across the deck that she was involving him, sharing him with the truckers, calling forth a sensuous accord in them all. She listened when the Greeks spoke boisterously of their wives and children, the gardens of vegetables they nurtured in spring and summer, the dreams they had for bigger houses and cars. She asked them about sports programmes at island schools, and found they knew relatively little, barring soccer for which they had a passion. The Greek national team was playing in the World Cup this summer and would certainly do well.

-And Turkey?- she asked. -How will they do?

Much table thumping and laughter in response. The Turks could not play soccer. They did not deserve to be in the World Cup. And then the proud, defiant statement that a single Greek player was the equivalent of an entire Turkish team, a variation of which Jake would hear two months later under more strenuous circumstances.

The songs on the juke box were Greek and Italian, with one exception. He put in five *drachmas* and, as the sea turned a pale blue colour near daybreak, they danced slowly to 'Helpless,' the high whine of Neil Young leading the chorus of Crosby, Stills, and Nash through changes in a north Ontario town.

The forty-mile trip took three hours. They climbed past some army barracks and a gravel pit into the hills, leaving in a haze of exhaust the Mytilene houses that leaned over the narrow road, often connected by bright lines of washing hung between balconies. On the other side of the hills the road dropped sinuously to a long, slender bay lined with pines. At sea level the pavement straightened out and ran between tall grasses almost tropical in their height and texture. Grimy whitewashed walls, pounded by years of traffic, marked habitations hidden just behind the grasses or on the edge of olive groves with their Kama Sutra friezes of trunk and branch.

Jake and Sarah sat at the back of the bus beside a small woman in a flowery dress who was holding two chickens in a wooden cage. The birds seemed less agitated by the bumpy ride than was their owner who held a handkerchief to her mouth and moaned softly every time the bus leaned into a slight curve or bounced through potholes that in their jagged capaciousness could have swallowed a division of tanks. A radio played music that sounded more Turkish than Greek to Jake, as it conjured up images of Rhonda Fleming and Victor Mature movies in which harem women in diaphanous silk trousers were fought over by lusty warriors in embroidered vests. A kind of repetitive and monotonous chant rode across the top of the amplified shouts and cries of the passengers and the quiet clucking of the fowl.

Every five or ten minutes the bus slowed and pulled over to the side of the road. A disembarking passenger would gather up belongings, discuss at length an issue of apparent importance with several people on the way to the door, then stop for a chat with the driver whose patience suggested that keeping to any company schedule was not a priority, and that if they reached Mythos by evening all would be well. Two or three times they went up dirt tracks to tiny villages where someone would emerge from a café or house to receive a package from the driver, and another animated exchange would occur. The first extended stop was in the centre of the island at the town of Kalloni where they were able to buy cold drinks and fruit, and sat beside a dry fountain while the driver shared retsina and cigarettes with some cronies.

-Do you think we'll ever leave?-

-Oh, we'll leave here, but I'm not sure the bus ride ever ends.-

Jake checked his watch. -If this is accurate, it's nearly twelve o'clock, and we're only halfway there.-

-Think of a sundial at noon. The hands, or whatever they call them, don't move because they never move anyway. It's the shadow that moves. No shadow, no time.-

He glanced at the clear blue sky. -I think the sun's getting to you.-

Sarah laughed, the juice from a peach running down her chin. -Want to hear more? No shadow, no shade. Sun-*stroke* at twelve on your head. That's how the ancient Greeks knew it was high noon.-

-Mad dogs and Montreal girls go out in the midday sun.-

-I remember in college History class how the English operated on Greenwich Mean Time no matter where they were. They utterly ignored climate and custom and stuck to the Mother Country schedule. Gin and quinine for breakfast. That's why they lasted as long as they did.-

-That's why they lost the bloody empire, too. Everything those British sea captains saw and touched and claimed was a tiny slice of England, just an extension of the ninety feet of home they sailed in. After awhile, things got out of whack, even the Royal Observatory clock, which, by the way, isn't at Greenwich any more.-

-Why not?

-After the Second World War, it was moved, because the lights of London were brighter than the light of the stars.-

-Time out of mind- she said. -Are you sure, Jake?-

Above Kalloni the height of land was spectacular. They gazed through the rear window across the whole southern half of the island, and thought they could see Chios on the horizon. What they could definitely see to the east was Turkey, a place that was a little farther than Jake wanted to go right now, although he knew that until 1922 Lesbos and all the outer Aegean islands had been under four centuries of sultanic rule. *Sultanic. Satanic. The enemy*. Was it Byron and the inspired struggle for independence that made him feel this way, the whole romantic defence of *the cradle of western civilization*? He recalled a novel about Byron's memoirs, supposedly written at Missilonghi, in which the dying poet extolled the Greeks and castigated the Turks.

He fell asleep, and woke to feel Sarah's hand on his arm.

-Don't move- she said, and nodded at the window.

He looked back cautiously, and drew in his breath. The driver was turning the bus around in the square of a mountain village. There wasn't much room, and he had reversed to the edge of a precipice in order to swing sideways into the main road. The back seats of the vehicle were well past the rear wheels and about to be suspended over the edge of a gorge that fell away for a hundred feet or more. Everyone on board was lost in conversation, and paying no attention to the process. The driver was yelling out his window to a man who was windmilling his arm in the direction of the cliff, as if the brink were yards away.

-Do you think they've done this before?-

-Yeah, but there's always a first time, too.-

The bus bumped against something and stopped. The chickens clucked loudly, and the woman beside them coughed into her cloth. Jake almost yelled out, but realized simultaneously thay must have hit a low wall not visible from their seats, and that the driver knew all along was a barrier. The man in front of the bus reversed his arm-spin and they turned slowly down the dirt road, dust rising in their wake, obscuring his view of the rampart of grace.

Their first sight of Mythos, when it finally came, was stunning. They were about ten miles away and on the north-west slope of the mountains that ran the length of the island. The sea was far below them to the left, and in the ridged distance the ultimate curve of Lesbos before the narrow channel that separated it from Anatolia and Homeric fable. The village sat on the side of the last ridge beneath a castle so imposing they thought they could make out the crenellations of defence in the shocking clarity of light.

-It's beautiful- she said, without any sense of cliché.

Jake agreed, but said nothing, hoping the mirage would not diminish as they approached, would be no *fata morgana* luring them, like Arctic explorers, to mapped extravagance of coastline that faded into air long before contact, with no direction home.

The final half hour of the ride was along the ridges and through valleys of terraced olive groves where sheep grazed, the bells around their necks tinkling melodically when they crossed the road in front of the stopped bus, the driver cursing this obstruction as if, the destination near, his schedule suddenly loomed large. They came around the bend and the chimera was still there, hundreds of white walls and hundreds of thousands of red roof tiles suspended above the beach and harbour, the giant castle appearing for all the world it would tumble to the sea at the slightest provocation of a tremor.

-Let's stay here- he said.

-Yes. For a long time.-

From the top of the rock, the vista along the California coast and out to sea was unimpeded. The road followed the water's edge for at least five miles, then turned up into the hills. The Pacific had withdrawn to the west, but Jake could see the surf breaking against reef tips that in the early morning had been fifteen feet under. Immediately behind him green vegetation hung over the rim of the cliff, and beyond that sheep were grazing on cleared slopes that angled sharply to the verge. He saw a cabin in the distance, set back from the road on a treed knoll. It was an old A-frame construction, and there was no activity around it, no cars on the track that led up from the shore or smoke issuing from the chimney.

2

The bus deposited them where the paved road met the steep cobbled street of the lower *agora* or marketplace. Various shops lined the route as they walked up, while wisteria in purple bloom wound through an arched trellis above their heads to form a shady roof. It was almost two o'clock, and the shop-owners were busy taking their wares inside, closing shutters for the traditional, three-hour rest period before the brisk evening trade. They heard a voice with an Australian accent and went inside a restaurant for food and information. The young man who served them introduced himself as Steve, asked where they were from, and told them he had been born in Sydney, where his father had driven a taxi for years. The family had moved home to Mythos in the late sixties, and the *kafe neon* had been flourishing ever since.

-This is the only place here where you can get decent food- he said. Unless you want to cook it yourself. How long you planning to stay, anyway?-

-For a few months- Jake replied. -And I guess we'll have to cook for ourselves most of the time, because we can't afford to eat out every night.-

Steve laughed. -You'll want a house, then, am I right?- And before they could respond, he added -I've got just the ticket. My aunt has one at the top of the village. Nice house. Two bedrooms, separate kitchen, indoor plumbing. Everything you need.-

-How much is it?-

-Oh, I don't know. Not much. I'll ask her when she

comes in, okay? She helps out at night. Is that all your stuff?- He pointed to their knapsacks, Sarah's small suitcase, and the typewriter.

-Yeah, it'll get us through the summer.-

-Too right, it will. All you need in hot weather is sandals and shorts. Maybe a shirt for the evenings.- He looked at Sarah. -You'll need a bathing suit. This isn't Mykonos or Bondai Beach, you know. No topless in Mythos! Listen, why don't you rest here, eat your lunch, and I'll go and get the key from my aunt, ask her what the rent is. No obligation, you know. If you like the house, take it. If not, we'll help you look for something else. Alright, then?-

They sipped their beer, and shared some slightly warm *mousaka*, mopping up the red-tinged oil from the plate with bread.

-It's funny- Jake said. -Ibiza was a tourist haven, but most of the Spaniards spoke only pidgin English. I come to the back of beyond and a find a Greek called Steve with a voice like an Anzac veteran.-

-He's a bit of a hustler, isn't he?-

-Probably. But let's wait and see what the house is like.-

They went out on a tiny balcony that overlooked an abandoned olive oil factory near the beach. A wooden wharf ran out into the water from the base of a sloping chimney. It was like sitting in the top row of a huge version of the Acropolis amphitheatre, only here the setting was thirty miles of sea and mountains, and the performance was unchangeable rock and water and sun.

-*Summer and Smoke*- Jake said. -*Suddenly, Last Summer. The Greengage Summer.* Eddie Cochrane singing *Summer-*

time. Sinatra's *The Summer Wind.* Have I left anything out? Hey, I know. He sang confidently, but slightly off key. -*We passed that summer lost in love/Beneath the lemon tree/The music of our laughter hid my father's words from me/Don't put your faith in love, my boy/My father said to me/For you will find that love is like/The lovely lemon tree.*

-Sorry to interrupt the concert- Steve said behind them.

Sarah turned and smiled at him. -He was just getting started.-

They went a long way up the stone steps, following Steve's directions. -The street under the castle. The house is more towards the harbour side of the village. It's shaped this way, like the Greek letter *gamma* on its side. He drew a sketch on a napkin.

-There's a low wall in front with a metal fence on top, and a grape trellis in the garden. Oh yeah, the front door is red. You can't miss it.-

The winding labyrinth of passageways was confusing, and they got turned around a number of times before Jake saw the arrowed sign for *Castro* on a corner wall. -This must be it- he said. They walked along the road for fifty yards and found the house. There was a rose bush in the garden whose perfume reminded him of the flowers near the *finca* well, and some metal steps that led from the kitchen door to the roof. They looked in the kitchen first. A wooden table with two chairs, a divan with a thin, cloth-covered cushion, a three-burner stove with gas tank beside it. That was all, except for the small bathroom at one end, complete with open shower beside the toilet.

-Cold water only, I'll bet.- He turned on the tap, and a

lukewarm spray flew out to soak the toilet seat and test the capacity of the floor drain. -Better than anything I had in Spain.-

The back door opened onto an unkempt yard where a fig and peach tree blossomed in close profusion.

-Fabulous!- Sarah proclaimed. -Fresh fruit for our morning yogurt!-

The main part of the house was separate from the kitchen wing. Two large rooms, one of which contained a double bed and chest of drawers. There was an empty cupboard, and a round, electric heater, unplugged, in one corner. The room across the hall had a long wooden table that had obviously served the previous tenant as a desk. Broken pencils and scraps of paper lay beside a torn and coverless English-Greek phrase book open at a section titled 'Getting Acquainted.' The windows of the two rooms looked across the yard and over the red tiles of other houses to just a glimpse of the sea, but it was when they climbed the stairs to the flat roof above the kitchen that they saw what they had found.

They were above the entire village now, and had a panoramic view of the mountains and the sea. The air beckoned to them, as if they could walk out into it and never fall. A village on the far side of the bay would be at their fingertips if they stretched out their hands. Below them to the right was the harbour with its curved breakwater and four fishing boats moored in the resultant calm of a semicircular pond. Only the dark wall of the castle, off to their left, closed in part of the sky.

-Did I say 'beautiful' before?- Sarah asked. -It wasn't

good enough. You're the poet. What have you got to say for yourself?- She put her arms around him.

He was silent for a few moments. -Not a bad word. *How beautiful Thy mercy-seat/In depths of burning light.*-

-Who said that?-

-I don't know. Procol Harum, maybe.-

Jake sat at the wooden table in the second bedroom and stared at the blossoming trees, the whites and pinks of the buds like pointillist dots on a blue canvas joined by the darker solidity of the brush-stroke branches. The typewriter stayed in its case, and he scribbled lines about Ibiza, playing with images as he shifted them on the page. He wanted to say something about Elly in the water at *Figuerales*. He could see her best when he lay on the beach in the late afternoon and the waves were breaking on the sand, pushed by the north wind that swept down from the Bosporus and the Black Sea. The sun shone in his eyes, and if he squinted behind his glasses he could cut the glare of passing days between himself and her. He sent Russell a postcard, circling one of the red-tiled roofs, and writing on the back, 'Twenty bucks a month. Clean woman extra.'

The pages about Karen remained in an envelope. So much was intervening between what he had written in Spain and what he might try to write here. If it were possible, he would send her a flat piece of stone with *Bullshit Artist* etched in Greek letters, a sign that would surely pique— repique?—her interest in him, the words an alphabet she would have to translate, like the chapter of an unfinished book in which everything is mentioned but nothing is revealed.

He worried about Sarah, though he didn't say anything directly to her. They rested after lunch in the heat of the day, slick with the sweat of sex more often than not, and then walked down to the beach around four o'clock. There were lots of stones, but they cleared a sandy patch they had no difficulty in claiming as their own, since the all the Greeks swam before their big meal in the early afternoon, and the half-dozen other foreigners in the village kept their distance.

-High society- Steve told them. -You'll break into it eventually.-

They usually picked up some food on their way back to the house, did the cooking, and ate their supper on the roof. Afterwards, they took the long, thin cushion from the divan and lay on it in the dark, amazed at the depth of the heavens, as they made out star behind star, silent explosions of the Milky Way in layered light.

In the mornings he rose first and went down to the *agora* for fresh bread and yogurt. They sliced a peach for the yogurt and spread rich amber honey on pieces of the brown loaf. Then they sipped their instant coffee with canned milk, sitting on the stoop in the front garden, washed by the scent of the roses. He did not know what Sarah did when he went to his room. He did not hear her moving around the house, and when he went to get more coffee at mid-morning, she had always disappeared. He assumed she was in the *agora* or exploring the village, but he was afraid to broach the subject because he didn't want to defend his compulsion to be alone for a few hours every day. Then she brought it up.

-Aren't you ever going to ask me what I do when you're writing?-

-I should. I feel guilty enough about it.-

-Guilty? Why?-

-Because I worry that you're bored. It's just that I have to try to work, and the mornings are best for me.-

-They're best for me, as well.-

-You?- In his ignorance it was all he could say.

She reached into her knapsack and pulled out a large rectangular notebook. Oh no, he thought, I'm going to have to read this. There was a slight edge of fear, too, that he didn't like, a possibility of competition that hadn't occurred to him before. He steeled himself, but he wasn't ready for what she showed him.

The notebook was a sketchbook with thick, creamy pages on which were pastel drawings by what he could see was a practised hand—the fork in the road of the upper *agora* with its the grey cobblestones; slatted fruit stalls of fruit and vegetables, Greek shoppers poised above the produce; the whitewashed village church, its wooden doors pulled open to reveal a hint of pews and inner arches; *caiques* in the harbour, fishermen bent over their curls of nets on the foredecks. There were two of Jake. In one he sat at his writing table, his back to the artist; in the other he was emerging naked from the sea, the water beaded on his torso like a cuirass, his navel hairs glistening with salt.

-Where have you seen me like that?- he said, laughing and pointing at himself, Elly's likeness in Russell's *Conversation* piece swirling in his mind.

-Poetic license. I did you in your bathing suit first, and

then took it off.-

-Was it hard to do?-

-Not really. I told you I was drawing and you softened up instantly.-

He wanted to keep the sexual banter going. It was a defence against his own inadequacy, his failure to recognize her on levels that had nothing to do with his desire to be with her and to be alone. She had made it easy for him, and for a moment he thought he loved her.

-You need your time, but I need my own as well.-

The moment passed, but not as quickly as he would have liked. She deserved acknowledgement from him rather than from that perception of himself he thought he had forced her to accept. It was a real enough talent she possessed, and she obviously knew such creative expression had nothing to do with any praise he might bestow.

-They're very good, Sarah.. You must have been drawing before this.-

Yes, even back in high school. I did a term at OCA in my last year of university. There were paintings in my Montreal apartment, but I guess you never noticed.-

He recalled the bright Laurentian water-colours on the periphery of his vision the year before. He hadn't been curious about her living space because his focus had been elsewhere, and if he had imagined her it was only as potential inhabitant of the European domain he would carve out alone.

-No, I didn't. But I'd like to see them now. Why don't you get some brushes and paint, and some bigger paper?-

-It would mean a trip to Mytilene. There's nothing like that here.-

-It would be worth it, Sarah. You should keep going with this.-

-Don't ever patronize me.-

-No, I mean it.- And to his surprise, he did.

She made the trip herself, going in by bus, but returning by taxi with an easel, a large stock of paper, and a box of paints. The brushes she had brought with her from Montreal. -Just in case- she said.

She would come home with work-in-progress every noontime. Sometimes she would show him, but mostly he would have to wait for the finished painting. She was visually curious and responsive to everything in the village, capturing the anticipatory emptiness of a *kafe neon* when its denizens were sleeping in the late afternoon, and the hands of old women as they sifted rice in colanders on the steps outside their homes. She even did a portrait of the police chief in his special sunglasses that reflected what he was seeing and eerily hid his face from scrutiny.

-How did you get him to pose for that one?-

-Are you kidding? He gives me the creeps. I did it to keep him away.-

-He's harmless. It's those dogs of his I worry about.- The chief had two dachshunds that were known in the village as sheep-killers, having torn out the throats of three animals and crippled several others. In the Colonels' *demokratia* there was no recompense for the farmers.

Jake liked best what she did with the sea. From shallow tidal pools to the sheen of surface ripples and the windows in the base of larger waves, there was a way in which she made him *touch* the water with his eyes. If it had been fresh, he would have cupped it in his hands and drunk it down. Even so, her work slaked a thirst he had not known he had, and brought new images to mind.

Sarah also brought back a short-wave transistor radio from Mytilene, and they were able to listen to the late-night BBC news. This was how they discovered the seriousness of Greek-Turkish hostilities in Cyprus and in their own border neighbourhood. Steve only laughed when they brought it up. -Those Turks won't do nothing. Ever since we kicked them out of here- he declaimed, sweeping his arm in a gesture meant to take in the whole island -they've been complaining.

-I thought it was the Greeks who got kicked out of Anatolia back in the 1920s- Sarah said.

Jake kicked her under the table. Steve might have the accent and manner of a Sydney street kid, but his *filotimo*, or pride, was pure Greek, which meant there was also a considerable measure of Mediterranean *machismo* in his response to women who entered the male territory of politics unbidden.

-Listen, Sarah- Steve said, leaning over and wiping a smudge mark from the table in front of her -you need to learn your history. The Turks were on Lesbos for four hundred years. Anatolia was originally Greek, and they took it from us. In 1922 they slaughtered members of my family in Izmir. Smyrna it was called then. If those bastards try to come back, we'll kill them.-

They were shaken by his vehemence, and by the undisguised dropping of even any pretence of friendship in the face of a threat to his Greek sense of self. For the first time, they felt vulnerable on the island, and wondered what they would do if there was a war.

3

Perhaps it was the possibility of war, perhaps just the inevitability of drifting toward those who shared the English language, that prompted their relationship with two of the other expatriates in the village. Dave was from Auckland, and Anne, his wife, from Melbourne. They were in their early forties, taught school in Italy and came to Lesbos for the long summer vacations. Anne was a friendly, vigorous woman whom Sarah took to right away. They discovered a mutual interest in opera, and Anne regaled them with tales of La Scala during their first dinner together. She told them how a certain *diva* had forgotten her Italian lines in *Turandot* and had made them up, much to the delight of the audience. -It was a grocery list. Different kinds of pasta. They loved it.- Then there was the cocky American tenor who tried for a high C three different times while the crowd waited in silence, and when he finally got it the silence was thicker still.

-He deserved it, the bloody fool- Dave said. -Strutting about like a rooster before that. If he'd forgotten his lines he would have sung about the land of the free and the home of the brave.-

There was something of the rooster about Dave. He was only slightly taller than Anne and weighed less. As if to emphasize his presence when they stood beside one another, he had a habit of hitching up his pants rather forcefully and hooking his thumbs in the front of his belt.

-He'll do himself a serious injury one day- Sarah said.

But in the water Dave's confidence was astonishing.

They went snorkelling at a cove behind the village, where Dave showed Jake how to pinch his nose through his mask and blow the air out of his ears so he could dive deeper without painful pressure. He also taught him to arm a spring-loaded spear-gun against his knee without surfacing and to fire just above the fish, taking the downward deflection of the arrow into account. They caught *kefallia*, a kind of sea-trout, and fried them for lunch over a driftwood blaze. Sarah and Anne divied up the tomatoes, olives, and bread, and they shared a pannier of water kept cold in the sea.

Dave was supposedly writing a novel about his New Zealand boyhood. It was Anne's word, *supposedly*, as she told them, when Dave was diving thirty yards offshore, that he locked himself in his room every morning to write, but she had never seen any evidence of production.

-After all, we've known each other since we were kids. How about you?- she said to Sarah. -Do you ever get to see the offspring?-

-Sometimes- Jake intervened. -It's a matter of getting them finished first. That takes time.-

-At least I've read his books, before we left Canada. So I know he's for real.-

-You can't always tell, love- said Anne, as Dave surfaced with a fish on the end of his spear. -You can't always tell.-

One evening he and Dave were invited out on a *caique* that was setting nets in the channel between Lesbos and the Turkish coast. Dave had known the captain and his mate for years. The two Greeks had been best man at each other's wedding, and now were godfathers to the consequent eldest sons. After some preparation, the boat moved out of the harbour and turned north into the channel, the five crew members giving continued attention to nets and gear, while the two *exhennia* stood at the bow out of harm's way.

-The poor bastards have a time of it now. No fish like there used to be.-

Jake watched the crew at their tasks. Everything flows, he thought. They like what they do. -Is it really that bad?- he asked.

-It is. I can remember them coming in waist-deep in fish, and the crowds gathering on the quay at two in the morning, ready with ice and the boxes for shipping to Mytilene. Now they're lucky if they catch a few dozen. That's why we're here. There's *room* for us.-

Jake climbed to the crow's nest, up the rope ladder extending from the gunnel to the top of the mast. It was just twenty feet above the deck, but the view of the sea and the coast was expansive. The boat, which had seemed almost becalmed below, now rolled beneath him as if only loosely attached to the mast and threatening to break free at any second. There was a ruggedness to the island shoreline, and the waves broke against it in great rising crests that reminded him of the purling walls of water on Big Sur. Dave had told him of the seals that came to the cove sometimes, *fosca* they were called, that chased schools of tiny fish and trapped them in underwater caves. Apparently the water was too warm for them to exist in any numbers that would threaten livelihoods. The Aegean, said Dave, had just been fished out. It was a shallow sea, and big-company draggers had done most of the damage.

The crew set some nets and left them, the boat moving parallel to the middle of the channel and well inside the invisible national boundary. Gradually it grew dark, and Jake could see the lights from villages on both coasts hanging electrically in the air, illuminated for one another only for the past fifty years or so. Before that a darkness that stretched back centuries, beyond lanterns and candles with their local brilliance and torches and signal fires that flared up briefly and were gone. Then he heard a whisper he could not identify and saw the curved phosphorescence of the leaping dolphins beside the prow. They stayed with the boat for a long time, outriders of an impending storm he was not born to forsee.

It was not the weather, but the border cutting through the middle of the age-old enmity that almost caught them. One minute things were quiet and the next there was an elated exchange as the boat veered from its moderate course. They were headed straight for Turkey.

-Jesus! They're on to a school. No telling where we'll end up.-

-What happens if we get too close to the other side?-

-Too close! We just have to be over the middle line and we're breaking the agreement between these two idiot countries.-

More nets went out and the engine was cut. They could hear the slap of waves and the men talking in low, excited terms, and then something else as well, a distant, chugging sound that seemed to draw closer as the seconds passed. The talking stopped.

-It's the Turks' gunboat- Dave said. -It patrols the mainland coast guarding against intruders. It's fast and well-

125

armed with a three-inch gun on the bow. They won't mess around if they catch us.-

-What do you mean?-

-A couple of months ago, some Greeks down the coast went across the line. They got eight years hard labour in Izmir.-

I don't have my passport, Jake thought, or anything saying who I am. -What about us?- he asked.

-Not sure. But we are with *them*.- Dave nodded at the crew. -And they didn't kidnap us, did they?- He walked back to the wheel and said something in Greek to the captain.

-Come here- he called to Jake in a harsh whisper. -He wants to show us something.-

The captain opened a hatch and disappeared below. He came up holding an oilcloth wrapped around a heavy object. Laughing softly, he unwound the cloth, and there was a pistol so old and battered it looked like a museum piece. A few shells rested beside the round chamber, glinting, in comparison, like polished jewels. The captain said something in Greek, and Dave swore in English, clearly exasperated. -Fuck! Here we go again. *One Greek is worth ten Turks*. Or, in this case, a bloody six-shooter is worth a three-inch bore!-

The mate began to argue with the captain, gesticulating with his hands and pointing back to Lesbos. -Good idea- said Dave. -He wants to leave the fish and get the hell out. By the time they arrive on the scene, we'll be safe.-

-So why aren't we moving?-

Dave listened. -Because it's an affront to the

commander's *filotimo*. Better to go down fighting than show a Turk your ass.-

-Can't you say something?-

-You must be joking. They'd put me overboard if I tried to interfere in the running of the ship. Even the mate would support that.-

The chugging of the gunboat was perceptibly louder. The discussion ceased, and they stood there, the *caique* drifting in the current, the stars casting much more light than seemed possible for things that hadn't existed for millions of years.

-They must have radar- Jake said.

-Of course they have radar. And they know where we are. They'll be here in three or four minutes.-

The captain and the mate stared at one another. Jake couldn't read the expression in their eyes, but he sensed that, whatever happened, their friendship was over. Then the rest of the crew gathered around the mate and stared too. 'Greek tableau,' he thought. Sarah could paint it. Finally the captain spat on the deck. *-Aï sto diavalos-* he said loudly, which Jake knew meant *go the devil*, or *fuck you*, take your pick. He stepped to the wheel, threw a switch, and the engine churned once, twice, then caught. He gave it full throttle, and they swung sharply around, the white foam of their wake leaving a trail for any pursuit.

And the pursuit came. He and Dave huddled down in the bow, as far from potential action and as close to the island as they could get. -They're twice as fast as us- Dave said.

-But we've got only half a mile to go to the line.-

They couldn't hear the gunboat's engine over their own, and didn't have any way of telling how close it was until they saw it about a hundred yards back and closing fast, like a grey shark locked on its prey.

-They won't get us. By the time we stopped for them we'd be in Greek waters. I just hope they don't...-

If you hear the shot you're still alive, Jake remembered immediately afterwards. The shock waves from the blast hit his eardrum at the same time the shell punched the water fifty feet off the starboard side.

-Shit, they're trying to kill us, not catch us- Dave yelled.

Incoming, Jake thought. The Ia Drang Valley.

The *pop pop pop* of the pistol didn't have the same concussive effect, but it scared him even more. If there was any chance the Turks were trying to warn them, it was lost now. This was a goddamn international incident! How far could he swim if they went down. The dark cliffs of Lesbos were still two miles away. Would it be better to try it or be picked up by the Turks? Eight years hard labour! He waited for the second explosion, praying for the assault of sound rather than the oblivion of silence. But the silence was something he relished as the gunboat dropped back from the borderline. The Greeks cheered and stamped their feet.

Dave stood up. -Too bloody close. I need a drink.-

They didn't have to wait long. One of the crew produced some *Metaxa* brandy and they all took a swig from the bottle, though the captain and mate did so unenthusiastically, refusing to look at one another, despite the encouragement of the others.

-Silly buggers. They'll never be the same again.-

The *caique* slowed down to pick up the other nets. Jake helped Dave lift out the few fish and toss them into crates on the deck. By the time they reached the harbour, he was shivering, but only partly from the cold. He wrapped his arms around himself, realizing he had come closer to death than he ever had before, either from stupid violence caused by an over-zealous fisherman and over-eager naval commander or from drowning in a black sea. In either case history would have taken his breath away. The captain said something to Dave.

-He says, don't talk to anyone about this. They threw the pistol overboard. We heard an explosion, but we don't know what it was.-

-Will it wash?-

-It better.-

The police chief, an army officer, and two young soldiers were sitting in a jeep on the quay as they came in. No one seemed particularly interested in him or Dave, except the chief who, without his reflecting glasses, surveyed them as they walked past and up the road to the village.

-We haven't heard the last of it. Best to keep our heads down for awhile.-

Sarah was asleep when he crawled into bed, exhausted and still shivering. He pulled her warm body to him and tried to think of the dolphins, wondering where they went when wars began.

The next morning he didn't say much to her, just told her about the crow's nest and the fish, and mentioned in passing that Lesbos looked different from the water. He assumed Dave was doing the same, and wondered if the authorities would bother with them at all. It didn't take long to find out. That afternoon when they came home from the beach, carrying their bags of shopping, the door to the main part of the house was wide open, and they could hear voices from inside.

-What's going on?- Sarah cried, rushing in ahead of him.

-Wait- he yelled, but then he heard her exclaim from their bedroom -What are you doing here?-

Jake went in and saw the damage. The bedding was on the floor, and the mattress had been split open along with Sarah's suitcase. Their clothes were scattered, and through the entrance to the other room he could see his books and papers in disarray. The police chief was sitting in his chair sifting through a pile of envelopes that contained poems from different periods and the passages about Karen. He was angry, but knew he should keep his emotions in check, and show just the right amount of concern.

-Who are you?- he asked a man in plain clothes who was shaking an obviously empty rucksack as if it still had secrets to reveal. -What do you want?-

The answer came from every cop show and film *noir* Jake had seen, though the insidious tone was now directed at him. -It is for us to ask the questions. You will come with us.- He snapped his fingers, and a soldier appeared from behind the door of the other room, a tall boy in a tight-fitting uniform who was made to obey orders. Then the good cop seemed to take over. -Please- he said, pointing to the hall.

Sarah grabbed his arm. -What's it about? Do you know

what it's about?-

He knew the cop was watching them and listening. -No- he lied -but you should go to the post office and phone the Canadian Embassy. Tell them what these guys have done to our things, and tell them they've taken me...-

-Where are you taking me?- he asked the cop.

-For you wife's sake, I will tell you. You will come with us to the police station. But there will be no phone calls, not yet.-

-We're not married. What right do you have to stop us calling our embassy? I'm sure international law overrides your authority.-

-My authority, and that of my colleague here- he pointed at the chief standing in the doorway, glass eyes reflecting all -exceeds anything your embassy might claim.-

Exceeds. He wasn't from here. It was a dangerous word. A threat.

-Stay here- he told Sarah. -Someone will be watching.-

She didn't reply. Jake could see her anger and, then, when she looked at him, her fear.

They walked silently through the streets of the village. Jake felt as if he were handcuffed, though on the surface he could just be out for a stroll with three companions. Then the old women on the steps looked away as they passed, despite his brave *Yassu*, and he knew any cover story would be difficult to sustain. He wondered where Dave was and what his version would be.

He was taken to a large room with a window that gave a view of the harbour. The window was closed, and the room was very hot. The cop offered him a chair, then sat with the chief behind a table some distance away. The chief opened a briefcase and took out the portrait Sarah had done of him.

-When did you do this?- the cop asked.

-I didn't do it. My...the woman I live with painted it last month.-

-Why?-

-What do you mean, why? She paints a lot of things. He should be flattered. It's a good likeness.-

-Yes, it is. I'll ask him about the flattery.- He turned and said something in Greek to the chief, who scowled and replied -*Communiste.*-

-He thinks you are a communist. That makes your woman—the artist—one too.-

-She's not *my* woman. And what does communism have to do with the painting?-

-Let's find out. Are these your poems?- He pointed to the papers the chief had just extracted from his case. -Here's an interesting metaphor: *In dreams they beat/the absent feet of God.* You're referring to the *falangia*, aren't you?-

It was in a poem about the Colonels and the torture of students. Jake tried to buy time.

-Well, no, it's actually more complicated than that.-

-I'm all ears, as you say. Tell me about the complication.-

Had this guy taken a degree in English lit. somewhere? Did he read poetry on the side when he wasn't interrogating prisoners? The worst they could do to him was throw him out of the country, but he couldn't let them connect his politics to the *caique* crew.

-It's a poem about rhythm, about poetic metre. That's what the words *beat* and *feet* refer to. God is the ultimate muse figure.- It was crap and the cop knew it.

He smiled. -Perhaps the kind of interpretation they'd give at Oxbridge, but not here if I translated it for him- he said, nodding at the chief. -He'd be especially interested in your prose, all those stories about rock stars corrupting the 'Star-Spangled Banner.' By the way, which one is really your woman?-

-What do you mean?-

-The one waiting for you at your house, or the one in the story? Oh, yes, I've read it. *California Dreamin'* seems a long time ago, doesn't it? At least her painting is about the here and now.-

The questions bothered Jake, but he relaxed, confident he could hold his own in this type of exchange. This is an educated man, he thought. Maybe tonight I'll have a drink with him. The chief spoke suddenly, his words a barrage, his finger penetrating the air. When he stopped, the cop stood up and walked around the table.

-You will remove your clothes.-

-What?-

-Take off your clothes, now.- His tone was all the more insidious now for remaining pleasant, and the benign expression he had worn throughout the interview hadn't changed. The gap between art and life was suddenly terrifying.

It took a few seconds. Then his bathing suit, t-shirt, and sandals were on the floor beside him. He was breathing heavily, almost overcome by fear and humiliation. The chief removed an iron bar from the table drawer. Jake remembered Russell's advice about a tight pucker. He couldn't stop one leg from shaking.

-Last night. What were you doing on that boat?-

-We were invited, Dave and I. Just to watch them fish, and see how things were done. That's all.-

-What happened?-

This was it. What had Dave said? -We watched them set some nets, and catch some fish. I climbed the crow's nest.- Then he took a wild chance at a way out. -I fell asleep.-

The cop spoke to the chief, who didn't reply. -But you heard the shell-fire?-

-Shell-fire? What are you talking about?- He tried to look very surprised.

-At eleven o'clock last night a shell was fired by a Turkish gunboat in the channel between Lesbos and Turkey. Our naval station on the north coast monitored the Turks' radio and understood they were chasing a fishing boat that had crossed into their waters. Your boat.-

-How am I supposed to know where we were. It was dark. There aren't any signs out there.-

-And you heard nothing, noticed nothing?-

-Another chance taken. -I woke up and thought I'd heard thunder. I asked Dave, but he said he'd dozed off too.-

-That's not what he said. It doesn't do you any good to lie. The crew have confessed.-

-I want to speak to my embassy. I'm a Canadian citizen. You...-

The chief rose and walked over to Jake, carrying the iron bar. -He wants you to bend over.-

His stomach was clenched, and both legs were shaking now, as he felt the bar slide down his spine and over his ass. Surely they couldn't hurt him. He hadn't done anything. Yes he had. He'd lied. And they knew it.

-What is the truth? Or do you still want to talk about rhythm and metre?-

-Okay, okay. They chased some fish and we heard the gunboat. The next thing I knew we were running and the Turks were firing at us.-

-Anything else?-

-No. I just kept my head down.- He wouldn't tell about the revolver. It was at the bottom of the channel. Neither the crew nor Dave would mention it.

-*Endaxi. Exeris tipote.*- The iron bar tapped his buttocks firmly, and the chief laughed.

-He'll keep the portrait- the good cop said.

When Jake got back to the house, Sarah had cleaned up. The mattress was turned over to hide the split, and the washed sheets were drying in a slight breeze. His books were piled neatly on the table.

-Bastards! They took my paintings.-

-I've got them. All but the one of the chief. He says it's subversive, but I think he likes it. They gave me back my writing, too. Want to read a poem about prosody?- He sat down on the bed and began to shake again.

She rubbed his shoulders. -What did they do to you?-

He told her about the border crossing and the gunboat. He didn't tell her about the return fire in case she was ever questioned. He wanted to talk about his humiliation, but couldn't. He hadn't been raped, though the bar had come close, and he certainly didn't feel it could compare to anything similar they might have done to her given the chance. So he described the nastiness of their questioning, and how they pushed him around a bit.

-It was stupid. I was supposed to be a communist agitator who influenced the crew. I wonder what will happen to them? What do you get for drawing the fire of a gunboat?-

-Let's go and find Anne and Dave- she said.

They were sitting on Steve's balcony with some *ouzo* and salad. Anne looked upset, but Dave smiled at them. -Another ex-con, eh?-

Dave had been taken to the station right after lunch. For awhile he'd told them he'd heard nothing and saw nothing. -Not too bright, was I? Half the bloody island must have heard that shell explode. So I finally confessed.-

-Did they threaten you?-

-Naw. I gave them the whole bit in Greek. I told them how I wished I'd had a cannon to fire back.- Dave looked at Jake slyly. -One New Zealander is worth a thousand Turks, and all that. I think it broke the ice.-

-You silly fools, why didn't you tell them the truth from the beginning? For that matter, why didn't you tell us?-

-Oh that would have been the best thing. All of us questioned separately, not knowing what the others were saying. No, your version, if it came to it, *was* the truth. You knew nothing.-

-All the same, you couldn't protect anyone. Not really. You shouldn't have tried.-

-Leave it be, Anne- Dave said. -It's the crew we should be thinking of now.-

-What's going to happen to them?- Sarah asked.

-The boat's been impounded, and their license, which means their livelihood, has been taken away. They might never fish again. They'll be lucky if they don't go to jail. The law is pretty strict about crossing the line. There's too much at stake.-

Line. Lines. Jake knew they didn't compare, but he asked Dave anyway. -Did they take anything of yours?-

-No. Though they did mess with my personal papers and books somewhat. Tossed them on the floor and upset a bit of furniture. Strong-arm stuff. What about you?-

-They asked me some questions about my writing. I'm a minor Che Guevara, I guess. But it was Sarah's painting of the chief they kept.-

-A high compliment- Dave told her. -It's undoubtedly hanging in his office right now. Here's to art- and he raised his glass.

And big bucks, Jake murmured silently.

When Sarah and Anne had left for a walk, and he and Jake were on their third *ouzo*, Dave asked him for more details.

-Stripped you, did they? They didn't lay a finger on me, though the chief lit into me a couple of times. The other cop didn't say much, just tapped the bar on the desk when they got me to take off my shoes. Sounds like they had different plans for you. Lucky we had our story straight!-

They laughed a little too loudly, and considered throwing their glasses over the railing to the rocks below. Instead they clicked them together.

-S'igheia- Dave said. -Your health.-

He and Dave were closer after that. Good friends, perhaps, though there was no need for definitions. Weekends were still weekends, and Jake didn't feel the same need to sit down at his desk. Sunday mornings they would get up when the sun was rising and the sea was like a mirror, and walk to the cove behind the village, carrying their spearfishing gear and some fresh water. Going to the cove was like the proverbial step back in time. They passed the cemetery where most of the bones were kept in wall boxes, at least for ten years before the containers were cleaned out and the remains of new residents were added. Then they followed traces of sheep tracks, spotted with spoor, through waist-high grass and brambles until they came to land's end. There they climbed down a steep path through thick gorse that thrust out almost horizontally from the cliff, and stepped onto igneous beach rocks with calligraphic markings that slanted out underwater and veered off into a sudden blue Jake could not decipher.

They hunted mainly in the shallows, chasing small fish in amongst the shore formations. He learned to avoid the sea urchins that pierced his skin like needles if he grazed them, and could not be extracted if they went in deep, but stayed there in subcutaneous patterns of pain until the poison dissipated and they eventually worked themselves out. If they saw a tentacle quickly withdraw under a rock, they pursued octopus, and carried bamboo shafts in their belts with shaved ends to poke at the creatures and impale them if they could. He didn't like to tackle them alone because the weird sensation of the suction cups on his arms or legs was disconcerting, as if he were in contact with some extra-terrestrial rather than subterranean being whose additional release of blue-black ink threatened to pull him even further into alien scapes.

One morning as they sat and drank some cool, fresh water and looked out at the spot where the Turkish shell had whistled toward them, Dave told him of the novel he couldn't write. He had been raised by nuns after his parents died in a flu epidemic, and then adopted at the age of nine by a sheep farmer and his wife on the North Island.

-There were six other kids in the family. I was the youngest, and always got the short end of the stick. They bullied me a lot, but the parents didn't care. Once they tried to make me fuck a ewe.-

-Jesus, did you?-

-Lucky for me I couldn't get it up far enough at that age. But I hated them for it. I liked school, and began to keep a journal there, writing stories about 'mum and dad' and the rest of my family that would make your hair curl. Fiction more true than fact, though. As I got bigger and kept getting high marks from my English teachers, I swore I'd write a novel one day that would tell the world about what had happened to me. Of course, I gradually realized it couldn't be completely autobiographical, that a few things would have to be changed to protect the guilty and liven up the monotony of pain. That was what coming here was all about in the first place. We stayed a few summers in Italy, but it was too much of the same thing as the teaching year. It was Anne who suggested Greece and an out-of-the-way island where I could write. She's heard the whole lot about my past. Trouble is, when I sit down to put pen to paper, I can't get it out of my head and on to the page. Part of me wants revenge, and the other part doesn't want to reveal himself again. But I keep plugging away. I tried to write about the sheep-fucking last month, and cried til I laughed. If I ever get it done and out, I'll send you a copy.-

Jake didn't know what to say, except 'Thanks.' He said that and they sat in silence for awhile. But he knew the question was coming.

-What about you- Dave asked. -What are you working on these days?-

-Oh, a poem cycle about the police chief.-

-No, seriously, I'd like to know.-

-It's hard for me to talk about. I've always written poetry, and still do. I can let you read it, if you like. Things about the Colonels, the landscape, the intense combining of time and place here. I've sent some back home for publication, or at least to editors of magazines and journals. But the other thing is prose. I started it in Spain, and if it isn't autobiography, it comes out of autobiography. A fictional memoir, maybe. It's stalled right now. I'm kind of waiting for permission to go further with it.-

-Permission from whom?-

-From someone I haven't seen in a long time, and probably won't see again. It's a hump I have to get over.- Jake laughed. He hadn't meant anything sexual by it when he spoke, but Karen would have appreciated the irony. In more ways than one. He thought of the sleeping bags at Big Sur, and the rock. 'Humping the boonies,' the Marines used to say.

They talked about Anne. Dave had met her in Sydney while on holiday there. She was just out of school and working for the ABC, an assistant producer for a radio arts program.

-Assistant! Christ, she wrote the thing. Not much going on in those days, I can tell you. Patrick bloody White was dominating everything, he and his cronies. Of course, there was Judith Wright, as well, and Thea Astley's first book had just come out. Have you read it? All about the Catholic Mass. Those bits of the Eucharist stuck between your teeth!-

-Don't you like White's work?- There were quite a number of frayed paperback novels in the English section of the village library, left behind by itinerant readers. Jake had just read two by White, and thought them extraordinary, though how much they reflected the Australia outside the writer's mind he couldn't say.

-Yeah, it's a great read alright. I just wish he didn't work so hard at being great. Most of it could be said in half the time. You can't fill all that empty space with words, which is what he's trying to do. Not to mention all those empty Aussie heads. And don't worry, Anne knows how I feel.-

They had married three weeks after he picked her up in a pub. -True love, no point in waiting. Her family didn't approve. New Zealand was just an island a long way off their coast. A very small island. Stupid bastards didn't even know there were two! Anne came back with me to meet my mum and dad. Well, I had to play it proper, didn't I? She couldn't believe how much we crammed into such a small area, and how provincial we were. Still drinking tea on government house lawns and pissing our pants every time some

English royalty passed through.-

-Sounds like Victoria, British Columbia.-

-She's still the queen of Canada, too, eh?-

-Everywhere but Quebec. She stays out of there.-

-At least you've got a Prime Minister with balls. Gives you a sense of independence, I'll bet. Ours wanted to bid for London Bridge, but the Yanks got it first.-

Jake wondered what the price of Trudeau's brand of independence would be. The October Crisis in 1970 had been ugly, and if the FLQ had been banished, the sovereigntists hadn't gone away. More Canadians than would admit it felt the PQ would form the next government of the province. Of course, Trudeau's fabled personal autonomy had been compromised by his marriage to the supposed flower-child. On Ibiza, Jake had listened to a black American named Chas tell tales about young Maggie in Morocco. -There wasn't anything that chick wouldn't try, man. She was hungry all the time. We used to call her 'Popeye' 'cause her pupils came on so strong.-

-...almost twenty years, now- Dave was saying. -A good long time. No kids, though. That's my fault. I told her early on about what happened to me, and how I had something against childhood. I think she thought I'd get over it, but I haven't, and now it's too late.- He took a deep breath and tossed some pebbles into the sea.

-How about you, then. How long have you been with Sarah?-

-In physical terms, only as long as we've been here.- He told Dave about the high school infatuation and the reunion, and provided some details of the weekend in

Kingston and Montreal. -It goes back a long way. I guess you could say she's a childhood sweetheart.-

-Got any plans?-

-Not really. It's just a day to day thing. We'll see where we are at the end of the summer.-

-She feels pretty strongly about you. But you know that.-

-Yes, I do. I'm not exactly indifferent myself.- He could hear the defensiveness in his voice.

-And why should you be? She's very bright. Very attractive. And she can paint, as well. Besides, you've got this connection through time that matters. She was obviously in your head for a lot of years before you met her again.-

Dave was right, but it made Jake think about head space and how you substituted there, replacing absent figures with those who made themselves available. He had kept Karen, or at least his version of her, on the page, and she wasn't in his bed with Sarah. That was a vital distinction he wanted to hold on to. His relationship with Sarah was more of a mutual accomplishment, an overcoming of odds most people would have bet against, that he would have bet against even after their initial love-making. If he had no immediate plans, he certainly hadn't given much thought to them spending the rest of their lives together either. What he'd told Dave about day-to-day living was true. He was happy enough with it, but he also knew a reckoning was inevitable.

Getting down from the rock was harder than he'd ever imagined. There were moments when he was afraid because he had to feel blindly with his toes for a grip beneath him, and, despite his age, he wished there was water to break his fall.

Once he hung precariously by his fingertips until he found the courage to slide the few inches to a ledge he could see between his legs. When he finally dropped to the sand he was covered in sweat and shaking badly. It was too early in the year to walk out to the tide line for a swim, so he sat by the rock and cooled off. Then he walked along the beach to the cabin.

4

The destroyer appeared in the bay in early July. They had been listening to the BBC news about increased tensions in Cyprus and the old-new dispute over oil rights in the Lesbos-Turkey channel. The Colonels were making a lot of noise about *enosis* with Cyprus, and warning the Turks of the consequences if any Greek territory was violated. The Americans were trying to placate their NATO partner, and the Russians were concerned about their Black Sea borders. It was a mess, especially given the depth of historical grievances in the eastern Aegean. Then one day Turkish jets began to break the sound barrier above the Anatolian coast, and the American Embassy in Athens announced that all U.S. citizens should leave the outlying islands, including the tourist mecca of Rhodes. On Cyprus, the families of American nationals were being evacuated.

Jake telephoned the Canadian Embassy and spoke to a polite attaché who didn't know where Lesbos was. -Don't worry- he said -we'll send you a kit.-

It arrived two days later, a manilla envelope with a brochure describing the rights of Canadians abroad, and a six-by-eight inch decal of the Canadian flag with an accompanying note: *Place Visibly on Roof of House for Protection.* Jake phoned Athens again and got the same official.

-How's the decal going to provide protection?-

-They won't bomb the house of a foreign national.-

-Do you know how fast those jets are moving? They can't possibly see something so small.-

-It's the best we can do right now, sir. In the event of

any violence the Americans will be sending a boat around to the various islands to pick up their people. I'd advise you to get on board.-

-I'll find a pole and you can stick the decal on it- Dave said to Sarah.

-Too bad there aren't any maple trees in our yard. We'd be okay then.-

The day after the last phone call, the Turks invaded Cyprus and a Turkish jet buzzed the village. *Buzzed*. A word from John Wayne movies like *Flying Tigers*. This plane screamed over northern Lesbos in seconds, and was gone before the Greeks could scramble their fighters from the Mytilene base. Jake stuck the decal on his hat. -Stay close- he told Sarah -and they'll know you're with me.-

The army tanks rolled in that night, taking up positions along the harbour road. Soldiers strung barbed wire along the beach and planted mines there. The most disconcerting thing was the arming of the villagers. When the Colonels seized power in 1967 they called in all personal weapons, mainly old rifles and handguns from the Civil War in the late forties. Those from Mythos were locked in the police station. That was why the incident on the *caique* had been doubly serious for the fishermen. Not only had they fired at another country's navy, they had done so with a pistol that could have put them in prison for life.

The Greeks changed. No more friendly smiles or greetings. The young men not yet in the army, and the older ones who had already served, took up posts at assigned points and stared grimly out to sea. The women rushed about, buying canned and bottled goods and hoarding them away. The bread was gone fifteen minutes after it emerged from the ovens, and delivery of fresh yogurt and *feta* cheese from the countryside ceased. No longer did they hear the early-morning cries of farmers selling their produce from baskets slung over donkeys' backs, and the *caiques*, of course, were forbidden to leave the harbour. Jake and Dave couldn't even catch their own fish to eat, as an army patrol dug in on the headland above the cove.

In addition, there was a curfew from nine at night to six in the morning. As the news from Cyprus got worse— many civilian dead on both sides—Dave and Anne suggested shared accomodation. -There's safety in numbers- Dave declared. -One Kiwi, an Aussie, and two Canucks are worth etc., etc.- So he and Sarah packed their personal belongings, including the typewriter and easel, and carted them down the steps. Then they retrieved their mattress and bedding, and moved into an extra room that contained boxes of books and clothes.

The days weren't the same any more. He and Dave gave up even the pretence of working, though Sarah sat in the garden and painted a young Greek with a Lee-Enfield who was stationed just beyond their gate. With her help Anne kept the house going, coming up with marvellous alternatives to lettuce and tomatoes for salads, and persuading Steve's aunt to provide them with the occasional hunk of cheese and bottle of retsina from the restaurant. Steve was gone, out to guard the nearby hotsprings from Turkish hedonists, according to Dave, but Steve's aunt didn't know or didn't want to talk of his whereabouts.

They played cards by candlelight. If they needed to use the gas lamp they had to close all the shutters in case the Turkish jets crept up, looking for significant targets. A lot of money in the form of toothpicks changed hands during poker games, to which they invited several Dutch and German backpackers who were stuck in the village. These guests slept on the floor because of the curfew, and left in the morning after Anne had given them some coffee, promising revenge in the next contest.

It soon became obvious that the Turks were going to win in Cyprus. The Colonels were held back by NATO from sending in their own troops, and they responded by cracking down harder in Athens. There were arrests at demonstrations against an ultra-nationalist in Cyprus and in support of negotiating with the Turks. The BBC mentioned rumours of an army rebellion in the north of Greece led by a disgruntled general who didn't like being outranked by lesser lights.

-Another civil war? The Colonels will invade Turkey before they let that happen- Dave said.

The entire Greek navy seemed amassed in the bay. They saw an aircraft carrier in the distance, and decided it must be American. The phone lines belonged to the military, so they were completely isolated.

-I'll bet the attaché's frantic- Jake told Sarah.

They woke in the dark to the sound of gunfire.

-Here it comes- Sarah said.

But there was a lot of yelling, and it sounded more exuberant than fearful. They heard the voices of women in the street, and laughter on the steps beneath their window. Jake went downstairs in his t-shirt and underwear. The front door was open and the gas lamp was burning. There was no sign of Dave and Anne. He put on water for coffee and called to Sarah to throw him down some clothes. A few minutes later Anne and Dave came in, half-dressed and arm-in arm.

-It's over- Dave announced. -The Colonels have fallen.-

-What happened?-

-As near as I can understand, the northern general threatened to raze Athens, and a whole slew of officers in the city went over to his side. The people took to the streets in the thousands, demanding an end to the dictatorship and a settlement of the crisis. When they saw they had no support, the Colonels tried to run, but they got them. That's what all the noise is about. Don't forget, this was a communist island during the Civil War.-

-What about Cyprus?- Sarah asked.

-Don't know yet. But if there's any kind of restoration of democracy the Greek nationalists there will be on their own. The Turks have won over half of Cyprus. They'll be happy with that and back off any Aegean claims.-

-Let's go for a walk- said Anne. -We haven't been out for ages at night.-

They went down to the *agora* and found the lights blazing in the *kafe neons* and at Steve's place. His aunt rushed into the street and hugged Sarah and Anne. *Tha inai kalitera*, she shouted over and over. They ordered a bottle of Cretan red and sat at a table by the kitchen toasting everything they could think of.

-Jesus!- Jake exclaimed. -The chief and his buddy. I wonder where they are?-

-They'll be gone within days, if they haven't started packing already- Dave replied. -The Greeks aren't about to give their guns back, and I wouldn't be surprised if there's not a vendetta or two to be settled.-

Just then Steve came through the door, out of breath and waving a rifle. *-Acusete!-* he cried -You've heard the news?- He put the rifle on the counter top, kissed his aunt, then grabbed some plates and smashed them on the floor. -I've been waiting seven years to do that!- He pulled Sarah out of her chair. -Hey, baby. Do you wanna dance?-

The village was reborn, a microcosm of the entire country. As they walked back to their house, farmers were leading their donkeys up the steps, shouting out their wares, as if they had been camped in the fields all along, waiting for release. They could see activity down in the harbour, a scurrying around the *caiques*, though it would be days before any fishing was allowed. A tank began to move along the road toward Mytilene.

-Let's hope they remember where they put every mine- Dave said. -We should stick to the cove until the beach explosions are over.-

The morning news confirmed everything. The Colonels and their cohorts were being held at the infamous prison where so many had been confined and tortured. A conservative politician was being called back from exile to serve as head of state, and a delegation of Greeks from different political parties had agreed with the Turks they should reach an agreement on Cyprus.

-Let's not be naive- Anne said. They still hate one another. And that island won't be the same again. The Turks are in a much stronger position, and the Greeks are going to have to live with that.-

They went back to Steve's for a late breakfast and sat on the balcony. It seemed as if the entire village was out for a stroll. Soldiers were lounging about their vehicles, chatting with young women who, Jake realized with a shock, were wearing mini-skirts.

-Look- he told Sarah. -Legs.-

-I'd like to move. See some *other* parts of Greece.- She smiled and rubbed the back of his neck.-

-It's alright with me. But let's go back to our house for awhile.-

-Yes, I'd like that.-

Later in the week, the four of them were invited by the *caique* mate and some of the crew to an evening celebration in a tiny mountain village above Mythos. In the post-Colonel festivities, the *caique* and fishing license had been returned. They were at Steve's at eight o'clock when a vintage Mercedes taxi pulled up, filled with laughing Greeks.

-Another one will be along shortly- Dave said after an exchange with the men. They waited almost an hour, and there was no sign of any transportation.

-They've probably forgotten us. After all, it's their country they're celebrating. We're not even cogs in the wheel.-

-No, they invited us, so it's a matter of integrity. They'll be back. Eventually- Dave added. -It may be a long night.-

Around nine-thirty the same taxi stopped in front of the restaurant, the same men inside, now riding a retsina-*ouzo* wave of considerable size. -They've been making arrangements. Everything's ready now.- Dave pointed down the street to a second Mercedes smoothly subduing the cobblestones as it made its way toward them.

Their destination was probably no more than three or four miles from Mythos as the Greek crow flies, but the route along the twisting mountain road was closer to ten. Even the Mercedes could not eliminate the potholes and ruts from the winter rains.

-Remember how your fairly-empty kidneys feel just now, and make sure you have a large piss before we leave- said Dave.

They arrived at the only *kafe neon* in the village, which was no more than fifty houses built into the steep angle of the rock. Above them, the dark shadow of a peak hid the rising moon whose glow illuminated the northern ridge. On the very top was an old monastery, uninhabited for decades and accessible only by donkey trail from the far side. Apparently there was a spring that had offered the monks some sustenance, but how, Jake wondered, had they grown anything up there, and how, in winter, had they survived the heretic Anatolian winds?

A whole lamb was roasting on a spit outside the door, and the owner was delivering plates of bread and olives, along with servings of fish and vegetables, to the various tables where men sat drinking. His young son was refilling glasses like a runner on an endless marathon. Once he got to the other side of the room, he started all over again. Sarah and Anne were the only women.

-Maids of honour- Dave intoned.

-Bollocks- said Anne.

-Where are the women?- Sarah asked.

-You know they never come to the *kafe neon*- Sandra told her. -It's a male thing entirely.

-Not on a night like this?-

-Not even on a night like this. In Greece *plus c'est la change, plus c'est la meme chose.* Politicians come and go, but the village women essentially perform the same roles their mothers and grandmothers did. Raise the kids, cook the meals, sit on the steps and socialize. Of course there are larger gatherings, usually for midday meals at other houses, and the church functions are important, but it's all tolerated by the men in charge, from the *pappas* on down. As for the mini-skirts, they're just fancy chastity belts, don't kid yourself.-

-So why are we here?-

-Ah, my dear, we're fascinating because we don't wear belts under our shorts and bikinis, and we don't *do* anything. Our only saving grace is that we're with these two brave souls who stood tall under Turkish fire.-

-*The boy stood on the burning deck/Whence all but he had fled/The flame that lit the battle's wreck/Shone round him o'er the dead.* Bogie said that in *Casablanca.*-

-Bogie?-

-He's confused, poor dear. Felicia Hemans' poem is called *Casabianca.* Ironic, isn't it, that he'd have to quote a woman to make a point about male courage.-

-Here's looking at you, kid.- Dave's voice was already slurred by the occasion.

They ate and drank, and drank much more. A *bouzouki* player arrived. Everyone got up to dance several times, and plates were smashed by the dozens. The marathon runner left off pouring and took up sweeping. There were toasts and more toasts, most of them to *elevtheria*, freedom. At one point, Jake noticed the *caique* captain at a corner table. When he raised his glass, the man's eyes barely flickered in recognition.

Dave leaned across. -Trouble coming. Stay out of the way.-

Then Jake forgot about the captain and was swept up with Sarah in the festivity. Great slabs of lamb were served amidst loud roars of approval. He heard the name of Papadopolous, the head Colonel, shouted out derisively. Dave looked away, and Anne put her hand on his arm.

-What's wrong?- Sarah asked.

Jake shook his head. -I don't know.-

Finally Dave turned back to them, and took a large swallow of retsina. -Roughly translated, they'd rather fuck a sheep.-

The hours passed. It must have been two or three in the morning. The crowd had thinned out, and there were only a dozen people, besides themselves, at the tables. The *caique* mate got up to dance, laughing and swaying with his partner as they each held the end of a red handkerchief between their teeth. Suddenly a voice boomed out -*Koretsi! Foboumis!*

-Everybody sit tight- Dave said.

The mate stopped dancing, and took the handkerchief from his mouth. The *bouzouki* player got down from his stool and slipped out the door. The owner stood still behind the counter, a row of freshly washed glasses in front of him, water beading down the sides.

-*Ti thelis?*- the mate asked.

Dave translated softly. The captain accused the mate of being a coward before the Turkish boat fired on them. The men at his table looked down, signalling their distance from this enormous insult.

-*It's fine for you to have a death wish, but you should have it alone, and not try to force others to die with you*- the mate said quietly.

The captain shouted -*The Turks know you ran!*- He slammed a thin-handled filleting knife on the table.

This is crazy, Jake thought, like something from *West Side Story*, only nobody was bursting into song. He knew if they ever started to fight, one of them would die.

The captain picked up his knife and got up from his chair. He held the blade against his pant leg and spat on the floor. *-Are you a coward now?-* he asked. Then, just as they had on the *caique*, the crew stood up and gathered around the mate. They gazed intently at the captain. He returned their stare, took a half-step toward them, then wavered. -*Aï sto diavolo*- he told them for the second time and, tossing some coins on the table, he pushed past the group and out the door.

-It over- Jim said. -They'll never talk to one another again.-

The party kept going, but there was a different tenor to it now, a sense of loss that came not only from the recognition that a violation had occurred on a local level, but also from the knowledge that this night of Greek *elevtheria* had almost gone and could never be retrieved. If you are lucky, Jake thought, the dictatorships in your life have to fall only once.

At dawn they linked arms with the crew and walked down the winding route to Mythos. Some of the Greeks would disappear and show up again at bends in the road.

-They're cutting across country.- Dave laughed. -I don't know why. They've got enough fuel in them to go all the way to Mytilene.-

The men began to sing, and Dave and Anne joined in, their voices rising and fading, sad and even mournful at times, with a slightly faster chorus that demanded they all take little shuffle steps together.

-It's from Crete, from the Second World War- Dave told them. -The partisans used to sing it in the mountains before they went after the Germans. It's about the splitting up of families, and the end of a generation of young men. I haven't heard it for years.-

The sun rose beside the mountain and was warm alternately on their backs and faces as they made their way downhill. Once in the village the crew went off to the harbour to gather their things from the *caique*.

-They'll be on another one this morning, you watch-Dave said.

They climbed to the castle and stood on the ramparts

that faced the Turkish coast. They were tired but elated, aware they had shared in something remarkable that did not belong to them, but was theirs forever by association. Just after seven o'clock, three of the four *caiques* sailed out. They could see the tiny figures on the decks, and waved to them as they turned north into the channel. A lone man emerged from the hatch on the reamining boat, climbed the harbour wall, and watched the exodus.

-Poor soul- said Anne. -He'll never get another crew here. And the talk will follow him as well.-

Back at the house, Jake and Sarah fell exhausted into bed. They woke hours later and made love sleepily behind the closed shutters, listening to the shrill sound of the cicadas and the voices of the children playing on the steps outside. In the afternoon he went to the post office and was handed an envelope with a Spanish stamp and an Ibiza postmark, which had probably been held in Mytilene since the crisis began. He opened it, not recognizing the handwriting, and found inside a smaller envelope with American stamps and a Vassar College insignia. It contained Karen's address and an invoice for five dollars American.

5

Jake stopped writing altogether during their last weeks in the village. For one thing, he felt, this was a transition stage, as he and Sarah prepared to move on, increasingly aware that their relationship was predicated on their time away from Canada. Divisions between Montreal and Toronto would loom large when they returned home, where there was a routine light to reveal contours and configurations not visible in quixotic reflections of the Aegean. But he was also stunned into silence by the potential for contact with Karen. In the rush of recent events, and despite his brief exchange with Dave about 'permission,' he was no longer certain about his Spanish fiction, and how urgent such articulation had seemed. What did he want to say *to* her now? Was there anything, or any*one*, there to write about? Given what he and Sarah had been through together, Karen's enduring place in his affections troubled Jake. Sarah was a fact, but he had never told her that he loved her, never felt with her what he'd felt with Karen on Big Sur, even if he could try to dismiss such feelings as adolescent, effulgent at the time, but surely dimmed by the long run. Struggling to maintain a sense of ironic distance from landscape and desire, he entered Karen's address into his notebook under the acronym BAC for 'Ball and Chain,' one of Joplin's songs that had blown the collective mind at Monterey.

Dave, on the other hand, seemed to have experienced a catharsis that night in the mountain village. He announced at Steve's one night that he and Anne weren't leaving Mythos for a few more months.

-We've got a bit saved up, and we've always wanted to stay through the fall at least. Whether we'll last the winter remains to be seen.-

Two days later at the cove, Dave told Jake he had broken through with his novel. -I can see how I've got to do it now, how I can distance myself from the characters but still give them my sense of things. I actually have this kid fuck the sheep. I was shaking when I wrote it, but for him, not me.-

Anne had told Sarah that Dave was letting go of something after a long time of grasping it to himself, but she did not elaborate. When Sarah asked him if he knew what was going on, Jake said simply, -Writer's block. I guess he found a way out.-

On the last night, they all went to Steve's. He gave them the central table on the balcony and told Jake and Sarah everything was on the house. -Not for them- he said, grinning at Dave and Anne. -They'll be around here for awhile yet. But you two, this is the end of your first stay in Mythos. That's very special.-

They had Greek salad, *keftedhes*, red snapper, and fries. Steve kept pouring the wine and saluting them in a combination of Greek and Australian.

-I can provide translations from the classical tongue, but the Bondai slang is beyond me- Dave told them.

-Where will you go now?- Anne asked.

-We want to see some other islands. The Cyclades, Naxos, Paros, then down to Santorini.-

-You should go to Delos- Jim said. -Of course, that means Mykonos too.-

-The Paris of the Aegean is your term, I think.-

-Too right. You'll see what I mean if you get there.-

-Then what?- Anne persisted.

-Home, I guess. The money's running out for me after a year. Sarah's got a job waiting, but I don't know what I'll do full-time.-

-Or where he'll live- said Sarah.

-Or where *we'll* live.- Jake wondered if emphasis meant commitment.

In the morning they met at the bus stop, and promised to keep in touch. If and when Dave and Anne headed back down under they might come through Canada.

-I've always wanted to see the Rocky Mountains- Dave said.

-So have I- Sarah responded.

They all laughed. -I know the feeling- Anne told her. -I grew up in Melbourne, and I've lived in Sydney, but I've never been more than a hundred miles inland, and I've certainly never seen Perth on the west coast.-

They hugged one another, and he and Dave shook hands. -I'll be waiting for a copy of the novel- Jake said.

-And whatever it is you end up writing. When you get over the hump.-

On the bus, Sarah asked -What did he mean by that?-

Jake looked back at Mythos. *There are no truths outside the Gates of Eden.* Sooner or later, he'd have to say something.

They went to Naxos and Paros where Greek families walked the waterfront esplanade in the evening, and the tourists were only slightly more noticeable than in Mytilene. The islands were dry and without the pines of Lesbos, but they had none of the dusty surface level of Formentera, rising instead in dramatic fashion from the sea. At least Jake thought so until he saw Santorini. Nothing they had been told prepared them for the black cliffs thrusting a thousand feet above the water into a sky so blue in contrast it hurt their eyes. From the boat the vertical rise was spectacular enough, but from the back of loaded donkeys swaying slowly up the switchback, under the loose tutelage of a Greek who could probably walk the path blindfolded, it was terrifying.

-Not for afraid of heart- the Greek said to them. -Is okay. Every day I do this.-

The far side of the island sloped to the sea, and they walked on the black sand beaches there, swimming in water that dropped away so abruptly offshore it gave no sense of depth or perspective. There was no up or down, no underwater topography; the fear of falling he experienced at the Mythos cove did not return because there was nothing to measure the plunge against. But there was another kind of trepidation. So level and unrippled was the water's surface, it became a dark sheen that absorbed all colours of their emotional spectrum. Exhausted from a ten-minute dip they collapsed on the sand, the black granules sticking to the salt on their bodies in malignant patterns they tried to brush away but could not ignore.

The people made up for this. Santorini was a poor island, and the tourist trade was just beginning to prosper. The doors to houses were always open, and it was difficult to avoid invitations for a *gliki*, a fruit preserved in sugar coating, and a cup of strong Greek coffee. Jake had never tasted anything so sweet as a *gliki*, and it was impossible to eat more than one at a sitting or even in the same hour. *Ehfaristo*, thank you, they would say, patting their stomachs as if full, to a whole line of beckoning women who would grab Sarah's left hand looking for a ring. *Yeneika?* Wife? *Yati?* Why not? They would laugh and scold him until he would say, laughing in return and rubbing one index finger on top of the other as a sign, *Nai, nai, siligo.* Soon.

-An orthodox wedding- Sarah said with just a trace of irony. -I'm not sure I'm ready for that.-

He had no comeback. There had been an increasing awkwardness between them since they had left Mythos and the protective confines of a life that demanded no immediate assessment. Here they were exposed to scrutiny from everyone they met. This included the mirrored selves they encountered in their nightly exchanges in a guest-house where each sound was potential family fanfare. They didn't make love very often in the day because they could read too much between the lines of their tanned bodies and had to meet one another's eyes without deception. When they did, she would turn over so he would enter her from behind, her face in the pillow and his above the bedstead, their climaxes a separate peace after a mutual struggle in which much was lost. In the dark they could pretend they were strangers while they anticipated sexual moves like twins joined at the fingers and mouths before the final intimacy removed disguise.

Mykonos was like a miniature downtown Montreal. You could buy anything, from the most expensive perfumes to same-day editions of papers from New York and London. It was a jet-set island, and the white windmills above the town could not generate enough energy to offset the electric presence of a French movie star and her troupe as they shopped ostentatiously at quayside stalls, or that of a Greek shipping magnate out for an orchestrated promenade with his very famous American wife.

At first, Delos appeared to be another country. An open boat ride across a wind-swept channel took them aeons away from contemporary film and finance to the ancient capital of the Cyclades, with its stone remnants of sun-temples and giant phalluses. But the star and the wealthy couple were there as well, having arrived on their private yachts. She posed beneath the nascent curve of what must have been the erection of a colossus, while the tycoon strolled among building ruins where the lords of Delos had for the better part of a century controlled Aegean trade.

-Obviously a lot of people were fucked over- Jake said.

The next day they were in Athens, and flew to London that same night. Perhaps it was the plane's compression of experience, the consolidation of intervals that would otherwise whirl away, that compelled him to begin. He started with the letter from Vassar and worked backward to Spain, the *finca* and the stutter of expression there. He tried to make it matter-of-fact, a journeyman's slice of life in which any grasp of design was restricted by talent's failing reach. The evasion was futile.

-You're haunted by her- Sarah said.

Jake blinked. -Maybe. Yes, I guess I am in ways. Though

perhaps it's not so much her as the time and place.-

He talked for an hour or more about California, about the music festival and Big Sur. She didn't ask him for any sleeping-bag details, but listened closely as he described the rock and the leap. It was only then her question came, and it was not so much a question as a confirmation. -When did you tell her you loved her?-

-Sometime around then.- He was angry at this revelation. -I was young, for Christ's sake. That was what you said. You did, and more than once, I'm sure.-

-The difference is I realize now I never meant it.- She hesitated for just a moment. -I need to know something- she said, and Jake heard it coming but could not avoid the blow or the one he would give in return. -Do you love me?-

-I don't know.- He could hear the lie in his voice. - Sometimes.- That was even worse, so he told a truth. -I'm not sure what it means anymore.-

-I thought we had a past too. Isn't that why *we're* together?-

-Yes. But I don't need to write about you.-

-What does that tell you?- she asked. For a moment, he was astonished by the possibilities.

Then the plane banked toward Heathrow, and they were out of such words. The flight to Montreal would leave in two hours.

-It isn't over- Sarah said, as they hit the tarmac and the cabin attendant welcomed them to the rest of their lives. - Between us, I mean.-

-Worlds in collision.-

-Collusion, too.-

He knew she was right.

IV

CAPE MENDOCINO

The cabin wasn't very big. From what he could see by peering in the windows, there was a main floor room with kitchen area in one corner. It was sparsely furnished with a wooden table and benches and an easy chair by the stone hearth. Shelves to the left of the fireplace had some paperbacks and various odds and ends on them, including a radio. Stairs built into the rear wall, and without any railing, went up to the second floor where a single dormer window and a small skylight suggested one bedroom and a bathroom. There was a generator beneath a shed roof for electricity. Faded tire grooves in the dirt drive, and spider webs on the window ledges and front door, implied an absent owner, gone for at least the winter. Jake looked out at the ocean, then at the rock where he might have died. Big Sur, Ibiza, Mythos, and now this. Places that write you, he thought. He would stay here, just for a while.

He drove back to Ferndale and went into the single real estate office in town. The woman there told him the A-frame had been for rent for two years, but no one wanted to live that far out and that roughly. Only $500 U.S. a month and he wouldn't have to sign a lease. He indicated he'd return and walked across the street to the Wells Fargo bank where he arranged to transfer a suitable amount of funds for a month's rent and supplies. In a booth outside he called his Montreal landlord to tell him his flat would be empty for several weeks, *and his department head to say he'd decided to do summer research in California. When he returned to the estate office and announced he'd like to move in right away, the agent was nonplussed. -Well, you certainly made up your mind in a hurry.- -Actually- he said -it shouldn't have taken me so long.-*

Dear Karen:

It's been some time, I know. I thought of calling you when I got your address from Vassar (the CIA could find you easily!), but didn't think I could explain things to you that way. I'm not sure this letter is going to work, but I have to try. You will understand, I'm talking about myself and my perception of things, not your feelings, then or now.

Something happened to me on the beach when we made love, then climbed the rock and jumped off. You entered me, and have stayed in me since, someone I have been with for only a few days in my life and have not seen for over a dozen years. It may have been only the green light in your eyes and the incantations of youth and landscape, but God knows relationships have been built on less. When I left California, I fully expected we would see each other again, that our efforts would somehow allow us to break down the distance barriers and borders of our lives to share more nights and days. That you were in my future, I never questioned. It was just a matter of working out the details.

Everything passes, everything changes. I live in Montreal with Sarah, whom I knew before I met you in London. No marriage plans or kids, but we've been through a refiner's fire that, for me at least, has burned for almost two decades. You may remember I taught at a university in the late sixties and took some graduate courses, but learned when I came back from Spain and Greece five years ago that you have to have more than an M.A. to get by. So I started a doctoral program and have now finished a thesis on Canadian poetry. I begin full-time teaching in the fall. As for my own writing, which you and I talked about in England and California, I had a third book of poetry published recently. What I've been carrying around since Spain, though, are fragments of a novel, and that's what I have to explain.

I didn't plan this. It just started to unfold one day when I was living by myself on Ibiza. The novel is about you, Karen, or the you who has existed in my imagination since Big Sur. I made up a Ferndale history, based on the very little you told me—of course your name's been changed— and got you/her to Europe and a meeting with a would-be Canadian poet. I tried to write more about California, but, except for some verse, a block moved in. I haven't been able to figure out if the block is you or me. I don't know where to go with it. Obviously the rest, after 1967, will have to be completely fictional. But it's a story I seem to need you to help me tell. I don't mean I want to use any of your experience since we were together, but I need your awareness or something like that to proceed...

It was both inadequate and over-the-top. He'd be asking for her blessing next, if he wasn't already doing so. But he knew he didn't require that. It was, after all, *his* voice he was inflecting. It always had been. He never sent the letter.

After Mythos, Jake didn't want to return to Toronto. The reasons for his leaving the city would still be alive and well there. Montreal was new territory where he wouldn't have to talk about Spain and Greece and reduce them to tavern talk of wet-dreams in Ibiza or Priapus in Delos. As for Sarah, she had her own versions of their past and present, her own voice that bound him to her, even though the apparent monogamy of mind she called love was at odds with the indiscriminate vision he was determined to protect.

They moved into her old apartment on Somerled Avenue, which she had sublet. His books and few belongings were sent from Toronto, mostly winter clothes and a few prints. On the living-room wall, next to the Laurentian scenes and a few of her paintings from Greece, he hung Russell's version of Elly.

-It's by one of the few *living* artists on Ibiza- he said. -I think the model was in his head.-

-Looks like your head is involved, too.-

Sarah went back to her city recreation job, and Jake was accepted into the Ph.D program at McGill. With a reference from the Toronto newspaper he was able to review books for a Montreal daily on a regular, free-lance basis. He worked on poems about Russell and Elly, and a prose piece about himself and Dave going over the cove dropoff to catch a glimpse of something deep below they couldn't identify.

He got to know Sarah's friends, some single, some shacked up on a semi-permanent basis, and some long-wedded with kids. He and the men talked about sports, notably the Montreal hockey and baseball teams of the late seventies and early eighties. He went to the occasional game at Olympic Stadium and was in the stands for the playoff home run that stopped the Expos' drive to the World Series in 1981. Sometimes he found himself in the middle of a backyard barbecue on a Sunday afternoon, rattling on about beer and Gary Carter's batting average, wondering if it was a bad dream, but never missing a beat of the jock-talk. He felt he could always recover his equilibrium afterwards when he focussed on university concerns. He finished his doctorate, and on the basis of that and his published work he finally obtained a permanent appointment. There were no grandiose plans. One year at a time was all he had in mind.

Sarah was promoted Director of Recreational Services for Montreal West, and had her own professional interests and commitments to attend to. They played tennis together on weekends, and their social life began to include some university people, mostly from other departments, who knew nothing about the Expos but a lot about René Lévesque's strategies and expectancies. When the unthinkable occured in 1980, and a *séparatiste* government was elected, Jake decided ambiguity was the better part of English-Canadian valour. -'Only cream and bastards rise'- he announced at a gathering that was part wake, part defiant minority assertion.

Since they never talked about marriage or children, Jake let himself believe this was a choice of mutual understanding, and one which he would not question. Sarah's "offspring," as Anne had referred to creative efforts, were still clamouring for space on the apartment walls, and he took this output as a healthy sign, though he also had the well-being of his own parental poetics in mind. While the Laurentians remained her *métier*, she occasionally turned away from real-life subjects to delineate those she found in books she had read: the rugged stone walls around Wuthering Heights; the consummation of an illicit relationship between late-Victorian lovers, their limbs white and flashing in a panoply of material colours. She was taken on by a gallery downtown, where her work began to sell. Once he asked her if she recalled her Mythos vision of him emerging from the sea, the cuirass of water burnished in the afternoon light. -Ah, yes- she sang in a Maurice Chevalier voice. -I remember it well.- Although they both laughed, he knew that figure on the beach had been contextualized by her present talents.

The extra income they now had was used mainly for travel. One summer Sarah did get to see the Rocky Mountains when they stayed in some cabins outside of Jasper where white-tipped quills of stone inscribed the cobalt sky and clear-blue waters of the glacial lake below. She did some sketches, and snapped his picture at the foot of a famous glacier, the slight blur of his movement merely a different form of moraine.

Jake stayed in touch with Russell. Every few months they would exchange letters and news. Elly had disappeared with Penumbra for awhile, maybe to England, who knows, but she was back and all was forgiven at home. The film-maker had sold off his property and nobody had heard from him in almost a year.

-Any B-lasagna westerns out that haven't opened here yet? Tuesday Weld with a tummy tuck? Did you see her in that flick about 'Nam heroin on the home front? Great CCR songs from way back.-

Russell also told Jake he was surprised he had never produced anything of substance out of Spain and Greece.

-Your mind must have been turning over in the *finca*, filled with naked visions of Elly and other delectables. Then you went into a long-term relationship, and your feelings about Sarah have always seemed to be mixed-up with that Greek experience that really hit you between the eyes. As for what came before that, you never told me. But obviously it mattered to you. I could tell some days you weren't letting it go. Maybe it's time to put things in the context of Ibiza, and even Lesbos. Who knows, you may even like writing the story. I'll do the cover if you keep the angst under control.-

Jake pondered the figure of himself in the Ibiza painting, and considered the possibilities. Perhaps if he were on Ibiza he'd be writing now, crossing paper bridges as they burned behind him, sitting with Russell in the Avila square, turning everything into art. He talked to Sarah about going back. *His* going back. For a couple of months, just to see if he could loosen up, telling her there were places he had to see again before he could put them into words. She did have some idea of Russell's significance in his creative life from the little he'd shared, but she wasn't happy about a solo trip, and he didn't blame her. Since their return to Montreal, they hadn't been apart for more than a few days, and she was certainly not adverse to visiting Spain herself.

171

-Anybody there I should know about, besides Russell?-
She smiled, but it was a serious probe.

-Well, there was a Miss Jean Brodie in her prime. Sorry,
just kidding.- Elly would be in her early-fifties now, and
Figuerales beach, from Russell's reports, was like the Atlan-
tic City boardwalk. -No, only me. I'm still there in ways.
It's hard to explain.-

-You could give it a try.-

But it didn't happen. And the place he ended up visiting was Montana. On a hot summer day, a letter arrived
from Ibiza, his name and address in an unfamiliar handwriting. Russell had been killed in a motorcycle accident
on the road between Avila and the capital. There were no
other details. The letter was from his sister who had gone
to make arrangements for the body and to deal with the
paintings and other belongings. She had looked through
Russell's correspondence to find out whom she should contact about his death.

-It was obvious- she wrote -that you were a good friend.
There will be a ceremony for him in Montana next month.
We would be happy if you could attend.-

He was numb when Sarah came home. When he re-
lated what had happened, she slipped her arms around his
waist and held him to her.

-You loved him- she said simply, with no ironic claim
on the word. Later she made coffee, while he sat at the
kitchen table and read her the letter.

-I'd like to be there.-

-Why? You didn't know him.-

-But I know you, and what he meant to you.-

-Sarah, I think it's something I have to do alone. When I was in Ibiza with Russell, you and I weren't together.-

-We've been together for years, Jake. You should realize by now you're not alone.-

-You don't understand.-

-Yes, I do. It's bound up with your writing and with Karen, isn't it?- She pointed to Russell's *Conversation* on the living-room wall.

-That's not Karen. I never told Russell about her. And besides, I haven't written about her lately.-

-Then who or what are you trying to protect?-

When he didn't reply, she told him. -Ever since California, you've carried your past around inside you like a child you're afraid to bear. Whatever our relationship has been, it hasn't been enough for you.-

-What do you mean?-

-I mean that you've seen my paintings, all of them. I haven't hidden anything away. And everything I've done in water colours or oils is inescapably bound up in my existence with you. I don't guard the borderline between art and life the way you do.-

-We're not the same. We can't be creative twins.-

-We never have been, but you're sacrificing us and your writing to what you want to control. In this case, it's your connection to Russell, but mostly it's a sixties version of yourself whose complexities scare you.-

-And things would be simpler if you went with me?-

-I don't think you want to find out.-

She was right. By excluding her from the Montana ceremony, he would keep Russell safe in a creative preserve of his own design. As for Karen, the gravid sanctuary in which he nurtured her could not yet be shared.

It went on for what seemed like hours, the accusations exploding like time-bombs that had been ticking since before the reunion, the sands of Mythos and Canadian domesticity not deep enough to absorb the shock. When it was over the sun was still aslant through the window, throwing splashes of light on the paintings and the framed consequences of their exchange. While he accepted the integrity of her assault, he clung determinedly to a *no pasaran* defence that meant neither compromise nor surrender. *In the final end he won the wars/After losin' every battle.* Fuck Dylan, he thought.

-Fuck it all- he said. -I'll be back in a few days. We can work this out then.-

-If you go, don't come back here. I won't be waiting.-

-How can you put everything on the line like this?-

-It's called a life-line, Jake. Not something you weave with words.- She went into the bedroom and closed the door.

-Sarah- he called. He started after her, but she had already turned the corner of a high school hallway to disappear in time.

2

South of Missoula, the Blackfoot settlement was strung out along the Bitterroot River, with wooden houses set on concrete blocks, a general store, and a lot of old cars and pickups. There were more people at the ceremony than could possibly have lived in the area, and some of the faces were white. Abe Brumfield was from San Francisco, and told Jake he'd handled Russell's paintings for years.

-If he'd stayed here, he'd have a national reputation. As it is, I can sell him pretty much anywhere west of the Rockies. What was it about that god-forsaken island?-

-I guess you have to be there.-

Russell's sister looked quite a bit like him, but she was shy where he'd been brazen, and soft-spoken where he'd been boisterous. -Thanks for coming. It means a lot to us.-

Jake looked around. -Everyone is here.-

-Yes, and now he's home.- She laughed. -He didn't seem like much of an Indian, did he?-

-I don't know. But he made fun of himself, not his people. And he knew their history.-

-Did he tell you he was on the AIM march in Washington in 1968?-

-No.-

-Well he was. But he got tired out before it was over and snuck into a fast food joint. We found him with a cheeseburger and milkshake, trying to convince the owner that a mural of the march would look good on one side of the building. It became a kind of trickster tale.-

-Did he do the mural?-

-Not there. It's on the Native co-op wall in Missoula. Have a look.-

The ceremony was simple. An elder lit the sweetgrass, wafted it over himself and the group of drummers who sat in a circle around him. He said some words in Blackfoot, and there was a general assenting reply from the crowd. Then he asked if anyone would like to speak. Russell's sister stepped forward and talked of his dedication to his family and people, how he sent money home whenever he sold a painting. She told the story of the Washington march and advised those from out of town to visit the co-op and see the mural.

Abe Brumfield came to the edge of the circle and briefly described Russell's prowess and reputation as an artist. -His work will not disappear- he added. -His sister tells me there are many paintings to be shipped back from Spain. We'll make sure the family approves of any potential sales.-

There were cousins, aunts, and boyhood friends who had stories to tell. Of the cow Russell shot that he mistook for an elk at the age of ten with his father beside him. Of the day he chained the bumper of a white boy's car to a school fence because he had been bullying Native kids, and they watched as the junior bigot floored his hot rod and left the bumper behind. Of how he saw Andy Warhol's soup can in *Life* magazine and painted a beer bottle in exactly the same style, creating an intricate logo with the words *Red Man* emblazoned on it. How could Jake match any of this by describing their table talk in Ibiza and subsequent communications? So he stood and listened, the memories pouring over him like paint that would never be washed away.

176

Then the drummers beat their deerskin and sang, people either danced or broke off into smaller groups to chat, and Jake drank beer and smoked a pipe that was passed around with more than sweetgrass in it. The Bitterroot Mountains rose up behind him, where Russell's ashes would be scattered. He had told his sister that was what he wanted. On his trip home to his father's funeral, she said, even though the light of Ibiza was in his eyes.

The morning Jake left she showed him a room at the back of the family house. It was piled high with boxes, old suitcases, and a couple of trunks that contained Russell's worldly possessions. -He wanted you to have something- she told him. -The paintings will come later. I could save one for you.-

-He gave me one in Ibiza. It's all I need.-

-No, there's something else.- It was half-question, half-declaration, as if she sensed the need was unfulfilled. -Take your time.-

He looked at what his friend had left behind, the unframed expression that the world would never share. -I'd like the letters I wrote to him, if that's okay.-

-Those are yours anyway.-

He looked at the open trunk in the corner, caught the gleam of polished brass. -The sax- he said. -I'll play the sax.-

Jake returned to Montreal and moved out of the apartment. They arranged by phone that he would do this while Sarah was at work and leave his key on the kitchen table. Though she inquired briefly about his trip, she didn't want to discuss anything other than the forwarding of his mail and the settling of bills. There were a few awkward moments in the end, but she cut through them by insisting she was busy and had to say goodbye. On the flight from Greece, he had told her that 'sometimes' he loved her. She must have grasped even from the beginning that his feelings about marriage and children would be much the same. He wanted to argue with her, to defend himself, but he knew that only a hollow sense of honour would be at stake. He realized that she was right about him, about the intricate and solipsistic nature of what he could not bring into the world. In their relations without issue, he had fucked himself and produced nothing of lasting value.

He took down Russell's painting from the wall, and looked at her Laurentian landscapes. In one was a fallen branch he had not noticed before, lying at an angle beneath the otherwise healthy tree above it, a few green-covered twigs still growing from its textured bark. It looked as if you could pick it up and reattach it to the bole, and the tree would be none the worse for wear. But he knew this was not possible, that wind or lightning had changed the shape of the tree forever, and that the branch would soon wither into dead wood and dissolve into the humus of the forest floor. She had caught the immediate aftermath of the severance when the leaves' calligraphy had not yet been erased. Closing her door for the last time, he fought to keep his mouth above the earth.

He found a flat half-way up the mountain slope and not far from the university. There was a café down the block where he could eat a croissant and read the newspaper on weekend mornings, and a club next door that had jazz concerts on Friday nights. A well-known local musician who taught in his faculty Music Department gave lessons for a reasonable rate, so Jake sought him out. The tenor sax was supposed to be a fairly easy instrument to learn, but the left-hand finger stretches were nasty, and even after six months, when he could perform recognizable versions of *Danny Boy* and *As Time Goes By*, he still had a lot of trouble with the low B flat. It was a heavy key that resisted his attempts at mastery, and it wasn't easy to reach an accord. But the music eased his mind away from student papers and his loneliness, and when he fudged a note Russell was there.

-How many white guys can handle the sax? Gerry Mulligan. Stan Getz. Then there's Gerry Mulligan and Stan Getz. Maybe you should take up the piccolo.-

-Name me one Native who's made it big with the sax?-

Then on the CBC, Jake heard the crossover music of Jim Pepper, an Oregon Native who played what commending critics called 'pow-wow jazz,' yet evaded their political reduction of his tenor in lyrical subterfugues (his own term) of breath and intonation.

-*Hey-yah, hey-yah, hey-yah-yah*- Russell chanted in 2/4 time. -What else can I say?-

So it went. The dialogue in his head he thought would never cease.

People die or disappear. You don't let them go completely, but the ghosts that remain between the lines are never fixed. They change as you change, becoming larger

179

as you grow, a true life of your spirit, and if you're lucky, a reason to believe in yourself and your work. If not, they shrink, like you and your words, into tiny replicas of what you were together, amulets of memory you hawk on streetcorners of the page. Jake had a lot of conversations through the years with Russell, Elly, and Sarah, or something he continued to call by their names, before he understood this. Gradually, he began to accept how much he owed the past, not to demand allegiance from it.

After many false starts, Karen became an unnamed protagonist from Carmel who grew up on Big Sur beaches and, following childhood and adolescence, a poet who met a young Canadian jazz musician in San Francisco. They went to Monterey Pop together, and to Big Sur, but it was she who became haunted by their moments on the sand and rock, and who tried to write about it for years after he had drifted away into eastern clubs and more elusive venues.

Jake persevered between classes and grading, and during his vacations, forging a rough draft in which she travelled to Lesbos and had an affair with a Greek painter, reinscribing the Mediterranean ethos to accommodate her woman's view of men and art with which he often disagreed, but which opened him to new perceptions and new doubts about his partitioned poems of the past. She was a romantic but not a sentimentalist, and could be very strong. There was something of Sarah in her, as he admired and resented her strength simultaneously, and whenever he tried to check her expression and behaviour, especially regarding the musician, he knew he was beguiling her, writing autobiography rather than respecting the novel voice she was trying to find.

The invitation to Arcata came out of the blue, and when he looked for it on a map, he was surprised to find the town only thirty miles north of Ferndale. Humboldt State College, a liberal arts college, made up half the local population of fifteen thousand during the school year. His plane stopped briefly in Detroit, and Jake's seat-mate on the flight to the coast was a doctor returning to California with her children to visit family.

-Yes, I remember- she said, when he told her his destination. -The marijuana capital of the world.-

He didn't find out about the quality of grass at the conference, but the local micro-breweries had their stock on display, and the beer not only had a sharper bite than the natural ales he was used to, but also cost just $2.00 American a bottle. When he went into a bar on the main square with some colleagues and ordered a shot of whiskey on the rocks, the woman behind the counter dropped a couple of very small cubes in a very large tumbler and filled it to the brim with Johnny Walker.

Jake blinked. -That's a little more than I get back home-

-Welcome to California.-

She was thin and dark, and her chronicles were locked away from him, but it was Karen's coastal tones he heard, melding with those of his writer. He had been contemplating a trip to Big Sur, but had that territory down on paper, and didn't want to interfere. Arcata was less than an hour from Ferndale and Cape Mendocino, part of her real life before his revisions began. It won't take long, he thought, and cancelled his plane ticket to San Francisco.

3

There was a lot of fog around the cabin. It rolled in without fail around four in the afternoon, obliterating the sun on good days, and adding to the gloom of drizzle and damp on bad ones. Jake hiked along the beach, finding broken lobster traps, bits of sea glass, and old, corked bottles, the latter without any messages from shipwrecked crew or passengers, though he did discover the wheel from a sail-boat, in pristine condition, so it couldn't have been in the water for more than a week, the name *Saugeen* engraved in a brass plate at its centre. He listened to news reports, and phoned the local coast guard station to tell them about the wheel, but there were no reports of missing vessels to sat-isfy his curiosity.

He missed his sax and went into Eureka looking for a cheap instrument on which to practice. In a music shop off the main street, he bought a used alto, revelling in its light weight and the ease with which he could reach the high and low notes since the keys were set so close together. But it lacked the timbre and depth of the tenor, and made *Danny Boy* sound as if it were being sung by Julio Iglesias rather than John McCormack. Nevertheless, he played in front of the fire when the afternoon fog had settled in, and some-times late at night when he couldn't sleep and the silence in the surrounding woods created spaces he didn't want to explore.

Every morning he would make coffee and sit at the bat-tered wooden table with a pencil and a pad of foolscap he had purchased in Ferndale. His lap-top was in Montreal, and this archaic manner of articulation slowed things down, taking him back to his first attempts at poetry and the smudged lines of these efforts that did not vanish into cyberspace at the touch of a finger. He had intended Cape Mendocino as a lure, a topography of desire for his writer, but she came unreluctantly and with a sense of purpose, a woman whose artistic reputation was based on her dulcet appraisals of human relationships, seeking new ways to compose herself.

She discovered her musician's whereabouts in the same Eureka store where Jake had purchased the sax. In trying to write about him, she felt she should at least listen to some jazz, which she had not done in many years. Flipping through the selections she was astonished to find his name on three albums produced during the last decade. The store owner, when she sought his advice, was equally amazed that she had known the horn player in his younger days.

-Do you have anything on tape- he asked eagerly.

-No. It's in my head. What he said. Not his music. I used to listen to that in clubs, but I never imagined this kind of success. He wanted to play, that's all.-

-Wow! You know, *Jazz Beat* would love to do an interview with you. I know a guy who knows the editor.-

She laughed. -Oh no. We were both too young to realize what we were saying to one another. I certainly wouldn't want him talking about me.- Then she wondered if he had heard of her. Were there any discussions with bookstore clerks about his youthful affair with a poet of later renown? Given his prominence, there was no reason to mention her.

But somehow this brought him into closer focus. -Here's my mailing address- she said to the owner, and asked him to send along news of new music and any articles that might come out.

-There's a *Jazz Beat* piece from a couple of years back. I'll dig it up and make you a copy.-

-Thanks.- She paid for the cassettes and bought an illustrated paperback on the history of jazz with a picture of Coltrane on the cover.

In the cabin she was dazzled by the lyric force of his playing. She particularly liked a Duke Ellington tune called *I Got It Bad (And That Ain't Good)*, which opened with a few gentle piano chords and then a sweeping sax uptake that led her into smoky rooms where the body movements of *film noir* characters were rhythmic and erotically charged, as they delicately carressed words and each other one moment and wantonly embraced sound and sense the next. She heard his rendition of Black spirituals like *Nobody Knows the Trouble I've Seen* and *Swing Low, Sweet Chariot*, and marvelled at the subtlety of his touch, singing along with him in the dark, humming the melody when she forgot the lines, the wooden ceiling beams resonating with their exchange. But her favourite was his version of a haunting Native-American ballad titled *Remembrance*, wherein mood and measure scored the palimpsest of her red and listening heart.

She put all this into her novel, Jake retracing her steps as she went along, the difference being it was Coltrane he heard on the Ellington tune, and Archie Shepp and Jim

Pepper sounding their heritage on levels of aching intensity he had not felt possible, part of a communal existence only they could explain. Nonetheless, he felt this was the way he could accompany her. She was leading him according to her abilities and aspirations, and music, as it once had been, was part of them again.

One morning she went into Ferndale for the mail and found the *Jazz Beat* article waiting. She read it in the cafe, her coffee growing cold as her fingers drifted down to the cup handle, hovered, then came back to her face, grazing her chin and cheeks softly in thought. The absence of a photo disappointed her at first. There were reproductions of paintings she did not recognize on the cassette covers, but as his portrait began to emerge from the critic's description of his music and performances, she became more confident in her own rendition of his features.

He was still thin, with a strong jaw, Roman nose, and slightly crooked bottom teeth. His fine hair had always been long, and he pushed it behind his ears when he played, a gesture she recalled attending any passionate involvement with a subject. It was obvious from the critic's praise that he was very good. He had jammed with some of the great instrumentalists of the day, and had a large following on the east coast, though clubs all over the country were eager to host him and his group. He had moved to the U.S. in the early seventies, was based in New York, but continued to perform at Canadian festivals and had a standing engagement at a Montreal lounge every year. There was nothing said about his private life, and she felt some relief at that, preferring her own inventions that prefigured his exclusive appearance on her stage.

Jake was subsumed by her presence, and by her attempts at balance on the high wire between experience and expression. He knew they would have to meet again, she and her musician, and he was worried about the result, recognizing that she, as he did, wrote because there was nothing else to be done to assuage the intervening years. But what would each of them say at the confluence of their respective tightropes, not to mention the consummation of their relationship?

At the end of the article was a handwritten note from the Eureka store owner. *He's booked in San Fran. next month. I'll find out the details for you.* She put her head down in her arms folded on the table, and stayed there long enough for the waiter to come over and ask if anything was wrong.

-No. Thanks. I've just got some news.- *News. Good or bad?* She saw him waiting. -I don't know yet.-

-Okay- he said. -Have another coffee. On me.-

She didn't visit Eureka for awhile. Good or bad, the news pushed her deeper into her novel, where she wrestled with her writer's emotions, trying to decide whether they should meet again, trying to find out if her book could contain the encounter, and whether her fictional self could stand-in for her in San Francisco while she stayed safe in a cabin on Cape Mendocino. After a few days she knew it wouldn't work. What he had meant to her years ago, and meant to her now, had to be confirmed off the page in a transparent space she wouldn't be able to gloss immediately with words. She wrote about her writer putting the pieces of foolscap in a folder and locking the cabin door. Then she did that too, and drove to the music store.

-Yeah, somebody else cancelled out at the Top of the Mark, so he's coming in with a trio for the weekend. Two women on piano and bass, and a singer. It's not something you just drop in on for the price of a drink. You'll have to get a ticket. Should I see what I can do?-

-Yes. And what about you?- she heard herself saying. Safety in numbers. -You'd like to see him.-

He smiled. -Naw, you don't want me along on this one. Maybe it'll work out, maybe it won't. But you have to promise a full report. Well, at least an autograph.-

She laughed. -It's a deal. And, thanks.-

Jake stopped right there. She was about to reprise their relationship after almost thirty years, and he didn't know how to react. The gender reversal —girl meets boy, female writer meets male muse—interfered with prescience, as did, to his surprise, ambiguous bars of music. Besides, the pages on the table in front of him, and those back in Montreal, were part of an unfinished manuscript he'd been carrying around in his head for virtually his entire creative life, and the stories in it had been predicated on distance and deprivation, on the persistence of recollection in the face of quotidian denial.

Suddenly *his* novel seemed a potential grave for memory, a crypt for everything that had brought him here, winding his way from Big Sur to Montreal to Ibiza and Lesbos and back to Montreal and California again. Karen had been a crucial part of that journey because of the undeviating nature of his pilgrimage despite its geographical twists and turns. Was he burying her in fiction where she was never directly mentioned, part of an internment process in which resurrection for writers and their surrogates was a ruse? What would happen if he tried to roll away the stone at the entrance? 'The borderline between art and life,' Sarah had said. He put the foolscap in a folder and locked the cabin door.

Jake walked down to the end of the beach where he hadn't set foot since his first day at the Cape. The tide was coming in hard, and he watched the currents swirl around the base of the rock before he waded through the shallows and started to swim. The water was cold this far north, and his shorts and t-shirt offered little protection. Ten minutes would be his limit before the onset of hypothermia. He tried to imagine the delineations of sand and smaller boulders on what had become ocean floor, but was forced to concentrate on his landing point and fight the constant southwest drift. Getting out wasn't easy, as the sea pushed him against the rough stone then pulled him from it, and the handholds were slick and recessive. But eventually he hauled himself up and began to climb.

It wasn't the top he had to reach. He'd been there before. Everything seemed familiar along the way, as his hands and feet moved in tandem, and he felt they would tell him when to stop, when he had found that height again. So absorbed was he in the ascent, the rock inches from his eyes, the contours and clefts so intimate in their assessment of his grip, that he didn't notice the fog surrounding him. Then he felt the chill, and could see no more than a few feet beyond his grasp. He turned his head and met a wall of whiteness. There was no coast behind him and no water below when he looked down, though he could hear the waves, and the occasional cry of a gull that pierced the mist. He hung there, his fingers and calves cramping, then slowly negotiated the space remaining until he faced the empty air.

He had no idea who Karen really was, but a figure as close to her as he would ever get was about to leap from the security of her words into circumstance she could no longer predict or apprehend. The only way he could let her go was to leap as well, his faith, like hers, based on what had been. It was never meant to be entirely blind, so he looked hard at the white page in front of him. And stepped through.

Back in the sixties, she'd been tossed out of the Mark Hopkins Hotel lobby while waiting for the elevator to take her to the top-floor bar that offered a wrap-around view of the city. *Asked to leave* was more truthful, though it felt like she'd been given the heave-ho, because of her jeans and tie-dye sweatshirt. Now she stepped confidently up to the front desk in Levis and a leather jacket and asked for a room.

-Yes, m'am- said the clerk, who appeared to be wearing the same nondescript uniform as the one who had shown her the door. -Smoking or non-smoking?-

It was a large and comfortable room, with a strange entrance hallway lined by decorated screens, and old-fashioned porcelain knobs on the sink and bathtubs. The window faced northwest to the Golden Gate and the highway she had driven down that morning. In mid-afternoon, after a nap, she went cross-town by cab to the City Lights Bookstore in North Beach and browsed for an hour. Her volume of selected poems was prominently displayed in that its cover was one of those facing out amidst a row of spines in the verse section. Pleased at this, she picked up a copy, as she always did in such circumstances, to reaffirm anonymously her creative efforts. Turning the pages, she knew what she was seeking. A short, early piece she used as an epigraph for each public reading.

> *In the room*
> *the tables are set*
> *& the sax player*
> *is looking for chords*
>
> *the lovers*
> *are at the window*
> *waiting for the night*
>
> *I think I will buy*
> *this room*
> *the lovers*
> *& the night*
> *the sax player*
> *is not for sale*

Suddenly she couldn't recall what the boy looked like

or hear the signature tune with which he closed his sets. She took the ticket from her pocket. Twenty-five dollars. That would get her into the room with the other music lovers. As for the rest of the night with the sax player and three women, the price would be impossibly high. Gazing over the top of the bookshelf, she met the eyes of someone she thought she recognized. Another writer? Someone she had read when she was young? She dropped the ticket in the aisle and walked out of the store.

Jake watched her go, and for a long time he fell, trying to brace himself for the impact, claimed by silence and the absence of earth or sky. Just before he hit the water, he cried out, or thought he did, her name, his own, it did not matter. His mouth was open as he went under, and the sea filled him with the shape of that penultimate sound.

Russell had told him that content was only the beginning, just a glimpse of what you were trying to do. They had been sitting on the stoop of his *finca*, the patina of almond blossoms shimmering slightly in the haze, the engines of their bikes ticking in the heat, cooling slowly from their wild ride through the valley.

-Those women I draw. It's like being allowed to see a toenail, for Christ's sake, or a tiny mole on a shoulder blade.-

-Angels on the head of a pin.-

-And the pin's in the dark, and you're fumbling with your lighter, and your glasses or your eyeballs are steamed up. But it's too late to turn around, you know what I mean?-

-Is that why you put yourself in some of the paintings?-

-Yeah. It's all about reflection. The eye of the storm.-
-*Don't look back.* Zimmerman. 1965.-
-You don't believe that.-
-Not for a moment.-

It had been sunny for three days. Now it was gray, except for the green light of the oaks across the street. She went back into the store, to where the ticket was lying. She looked around, but the other writer was gone. She was on her own.

He came up, gasping for air, the fog a second sea in which he swam; his head, like the rest of his body, except for his arms, invisible to him; no compass but his own breathing as he listened for the shore. He remembered the current previously pulling him outward, felt the tug now, and the direction in which he must be moving. It wasn't strong, but it was deliberate, so he began his counter-strokes of survival, hoping there had been no storied shift beneath him, that his sense of north and east into the continent would take him home.

CODA

Karen spent the rest of the afternoon exploring the town, passing the *bodegas* that stayed open through the *siesta* hours, and following narrow, cobbled streets with shuttered shops and residence doorways marked by brightly-coloured fly-screens. When it became cooler, she drove up the paved highway to a beach named *Figuerales* that had been advertised at the conference. Two giant hotels dominated the ridge-line above the sand, where hundreds of men and women in skimpy bikini bottoms lay on towels or floated in an area enclosed by pontoons that bore slogans for Spanish beer and cigarettes. None of it was inviting, and she stayed by the car for awhile, trying to imagine what it must have been like here when currents rather than currency determined whether you would sink or swim.

In the evening, after dinner with some colleagues in the square, she headed for Ibiza town. Tomorrow she would fly out to Barcelona, and from there to New York. Once, Jim would have met her at the airport, and they would have exchanged the stories of their week apart, sitting on the patio of their Long Island house where they had lived since she had joined UNESCO and he had begun teaching at the state university. They met as field worker trainees, and married before going together to Guatemala. A year later, their first child was born in the hospital in Rabinal where lay the corpses of sixty men shot by the *judiciales*, the government security force responsible for disappearances and killings. They journeyed to the States for the birth of their youngest daughter, and stayed there since their working visas were about to expire. Wherever they went subsequently, they associated their travelling liberties with the death squad term *darle passaporte*, 'to give someone a passport,' that is, to murder with official impunity. It was hard to believe he was gone, remarried and a grandfather to his step-child's boys in Iowa. Their own girls were grown, of course. The eldest lived upstate near her in-laws, while the younger one, in her final year at Vassar, shared a flat with her boyfriend. They stayed with her when they came to the city, teasing her about her independence and worrying about her increased time on the road.

As dusk came on, traffic between the stands of pine became less frequent, the tourist caravans having found their culinary destinations or incipient night-life festivities. She rolled down her window, inhaling the oleander scent and the smoky residue of wood fires burning in *fincas* beyond her low beams. At the bottom of a hill near a small white-washed chapel dedicated to the patron saint of the island, the car engine sputtered and died. She shifted into neutral and steered onto the shoulder, reminding herself that she had changed many tires, but knew little about internal combustion and its accompanying metal parts. There was no inside release lever, so she got out and began to fiddle with the hood latch, the sound of crickets in the background like a cynical chorus commenting on her ineptitude. Finally the latch clicked, and she lifted the hood to a position where it stuck precariously without benefit of a supporting rod. There was no moon, and despite the emerging stars she couldn't see well enough to permit any wild guesses as to the trouble. She looked at the chapel, dark and silent. There ought to be a phone for emergencies, she mused, if not to God, at least to his chief mechanic.

A motorbike roared by, its headlight blinding her momentarily, enveloping her in its glare. When her vision cleared, she saw the red lamp on its rear fender suddenly brighten, and heard the engine noise subside somewhat. The eye of light circled, and moved toward the car. 'Okay,' she thought, I might speak Spanish, but I'm alone, and there's no place to run except into a chapel I've just blasphemed.'

The figure that swung off the bike was large and male. He flicked on a torch that he kept pointed at the ground, and all she saw the soft glow were the cuffs of his jeans and his dust-caked boots. -Hi- he said. -What's the trouble?-

Definitely American, which surprised her. Northwest, maybe. -I'm glad you speak English. That makes it much easier for you to explain the story to me.-

He set the torch on the engine block, as she stepped aside to give him room, and leaned into the bowl of light, his hands already reaching for wires and probing various greasy outcrops. They were dirty hands, though it wasn't grease they were stained by, and the fingers had a fineness to their movements that did not necessarily rule out manual labour as their prime occupation, but which suggested something else as well. As he bent lower, she saw the strong lines of his features, and the ponytail.

-Could be a plug- Russell said, and went over to the leather bag on the side of his bike for a socket wrench. He removed the plugs, and used a penknife to scrape the dirt and rust from the points.

-It's paint, isn't it?- she asked. -On your hands, I mean.

-Yeah, it never comes off. After awhile, you give up trying.-

-You're an artist, then?-

-That's what they say.- He put the plugs back in. -Try it now.-

The engine coughed and caught; the familiar hum. He came to the window. -That should get you to town.-

-Thanks- she said. -Do you live on the island?-

-Twenty-five years.-

-Where are you from originally?-

-Montana. Just outside Missoula.-

-Too many questions, I know. But what do you paint? I mean, what kind of a painter are you?-

-Life studies- he said. He took a piece of paper from his jeans, and asked her for a pen. He put the torch and paper on the roof. She heard the pen rasping against the steel. When he had done he gave her the paper, and she saw her likeness behind the steering wheel, with the tiny scrawl of his signature in the corner.

She laughed. -Thanks again.-

As he lifted the torch down from the roof, the beam illuminated her face. -Where did you get those earrings?-

-California. They're dreamcatchers.-

-*Paap aa gaa noot sim*- he said.

So he was Native. That shouldn't make any difference, she realized. But, of course, it did. -The next time I'm here, I'd like to come and see some of your work, if that's okay.

196

Maybe with my daughters- she added, feeling foolish in her revelations. -They...Sorry, I guess I'm a bit of an open book.-

Russell smiled. -Me too, sometimes. But at least Blackfoot's not a written language.- He put the tools in the pannier, and started the bike. Then he lifted his hand in farewell, and disappeared into the night.

Karen sat there for a long time, the island around her like a memory she could not place. She looked again at his drawing in the dashboard light. In the corner she saw it clearly now, a miniature profile of the artist's countenance watching her reflection.

-Sometimes I turn, there's someone there, other times it's only me.- She pulled onto the pavement, and tried to continue with the song, but the lyrics escaped her. The car ran smoothly through the dark tunnel of trees toward the sea. Nothing is written, he had said. She would have to remember it all before she got home.